ISLAND OF
LUVENDERS

For your love, support and inexhaustible tolerance when the luvenders ran amok through our house—thank you Sean.

ISLAND OF LUVENDERS
= *June Considine* =

POOLBEG

Book Three of the Zentyre Series

First published 1991 by
Poolbeg Press Ltd
Knocksedan House,
Swords, Co Dublin, Ireland

© June Considine, 1991

The moral right of the author has been asserted.

Poolbeg Press receives assistance from
the Arts Council / An Chomhairle Ealaíon, Ireland.

ISBN 1 85371 149 7

All rights reserved. No part of this publication may be reproduced or transmitted in any form or by any means, electronic or mechanical, including photography, recording, or any information storage or retrieval system, without permission in writing from the publisher. The book is sold subject to the condition that it shall not, by way of trade or otherwise, be lent, resold or otherwise circulated without the publisher's prior consent in any form of binding or cover other than that in which it is published and without a similar condition including this condition being imposed on the subsequent purchaser.

Cover design by Aileen Caffrey
Set by Richard Parfrey in New Century Schoolbook 12/14.5
Printed by The Guernsey Press Company Ltd,
Vale, Guernsey, Channel Islands

Contents

	Prologue: S Gamble in the Tribab	i
1	Visions from Isealina	1
2	The First Quarrel	15
3	The Start of the Christmas Holidays	25
4	A Boy Called Rich	38
5	The Zentyre Meeting	49
6	The Spectrum of Vice	61
7	The House on Jutting Toe Pier	78
8	A Christmas Shopping Spree	93
9	The Cry of the Red-feathered Bird	106
10	Embellishing the Truth	120
11	Spacer's Strange Behaviour	129
12	Lucy Arrives in Isealina	148
13	The Festival of Merrick 200	166
14	Trapped in the Mist	186
15	The Song of Farewell	198
	Epilogue	211

A promise made. A promise kept. Three green stones will be returned to the river of Isealina. Elsie Constance will disappear, her ghostly shadow no longer hovering on the edge of his life.

A promise made. A promise broken. Stop the mud-flow as it slides towards the concert hall. Leave the town of Merrick in peace, no longer troubled by zentyre enchantment.

Prologue
A Gamble in the Tribab

hen Solquest returned to the island of Isealina, his promise made to the ghostly child, Elsie Constance, was like a thorn embedded in his mind. A thorn that festered each time he remembered the Cold Command Charlie concert and the events that occurred that night. At his command the mud-flow had ceased sliding towards the concert hall. His decision to stop the mud-flow had been inspired neither by pity or mercy for his intended victims. Fear of the ghostly child was the only reason he did not carry out his plan of vengeance. Solquest believed that a promise made in fear to Elsie Constance was a defeat. It was also a humiliation that could not be tolerated by a great zentyre. But he was unable to vent his fury on her. She too had made a

promise and, in keeping it, had disappeared from his life. He could no longer see her vigilant shadow that had challenged his power on many occasions. The force of his zentyre enchantment could no longer harm her.

His thoughts turned instead to the Custodian of the Dark Rill. For eighteen months he had been a prisoner of the red-feathered bird whose musical voice had mocked him when he floated in the rill's eternal grave of silence. The white eyes of the Custodian had glistened with feverish excitement as she forced him to gamble for his freedom. Helpless and terrified, he had been pulled towards the sharp Y of the rill and told to choose the direction of his future. If he had chosen the wrong side of the Y he would have been trapped forever between banks of dead trees and forced to float upon an endless, flowing tide. Upon such a slender chance of fate had the future of the great Solquest hung, a casual gamble to amuse the Custodian of the Dark Rill. She had played with his fear, laughed at his terror as he approached the point of decision.

These things Solquest could not forgive or forget. He wanted to crush the bird in his hands and wring the life from her slender neck. But that would be too easy, the punishment

Prologue

too swift and merciful. Solquest liked to plan, to manipulate and carry out a grand scheme, worthy of his cunning. And when that was complete he would once more turn his attention to Merrick Town. From his tribab, the enchanted cavern of Isealina where he lived with his army of luvenders, he would spin his zentyre enchantment and destroy the town forever.

As the weeks passed he sat in the shelter of the rocks that surrounded his island like a row of jagged teeth. The luvenders anxiously watched for a signal that would bring them scurrying to his side. But when they approached him his eyes were devoid of emotion. Only the deep lines around his mouth expressed the bitterness of his thoughts. They returned to their garden of mulchantus and waited.

The garden of mulchantus was a beautiful sight to behold. Over the centuries the forces of wind and rain had sculpted the dome-shaped rocky island of Isealina into craggy ledges where mulchantus blossomed, providing a rich harvest of food and drink for the luvenders. Row upon row of plants were in bloom, red thorns protruding from rubbery stems, bronze leaves glinting, heavy black-flowering heads nodding in the wind. But when the wind blew through the ledges it did not carry the fragrant scent of flowers opening their petals to the sun. Instead it caught the putrid fumes of decaying vegetation, a smell like rotting seaweed, rising from the heart of the blossoms. Above the top ledge of the mulchantus garden the tribab, covered in a slime-green carpet of moss, rose like a swollen boil on the summit of Isealina.

When the time was right, Solquest left the shelter of the rocks and called his army together. "Come, luvenders. Let us enter the tribab. We will take a small gamble and measure the odds on our success."

They climbed up a pathway of steps that was banked on either side by layers of mulchantus plants. They stopped at the entrance to the tribab and Solquest, standing in front of the mossy dome, began to chant:

> *Tribab!*
> *Home of the great Solquest.*
> *Bid us enter*
> *The root of evil!*

A panel of rock slid across to reveal a narrow passageway. Steep stone steps were cut into the interior rock, leading downwards towards

Prologue

the centre of the earth. The tribab was a warren of caverns and tunnels that ran through the island. Solquest lived in the central cavern, a bleak and frightening place, where shoulders of rock protruded from the walls and cast grotesque shapes on the floor. Rows of stalactites hung from the ceiling, gleaming with a frosty-blue hue. A rock squatted on the floor like a monstrous toad with a broad back upon which a hollow ball of glass rested.

The glass was dull and lustreless, its clarity dimmed by the trapped vapour that swirled within it. Solquest placed his hands on either side of the orb and it opened, revealing tiny, delicately-tinted crystals. They threw out strong rays of silver light, as if a great source of energy was stored within them.

"The crystals of Ulum," growled Solquest. The luvenders made gulping sounds of pleasure, pushing against each other in excitement. Solquest carried the orb from the tribab, followed by the luvenders. He emerged into daylight and walked around the highest ledge of the mulchantus garden, his army forming a long, circling procession behind him. Soon they had surrounded the tribab in a ring. Solquest stood in front of the entrance and breathed into the orb. The silver rays that were released caused the luvenders to draw back as if blown by a turbulent gale. The zentyre cried out in a ringing chant of command.

> *Crystals of Ulum!*
> *Crushed from the spirit of the zentyre*
> *Strong as the breath of Solquest's fury.*
> *Seal this tribab*
> *From those who would venture within.*

Immediately the silvery vapour rising from the orb strengthened. It began to fan outwards, covering the tribab in a mist. It was the same mist that surrounded Isealina in a clammy blanket of protection—and just as difficult for those without zentyre enchantment to penetrate.

"Let us return the crystals of Ulum to their resting place and then the gamble will begin," cried Solquest. For the first time since his return from the old mill the luvenders saw their master's smile of cruelty touch his eyes and light them with malevolent satisfaction.

Flying above the Dark Rill, the Custodian watched the strange happenings on Isealina with her mysterious eyes and remained untroubled. She did not feel emotions like revenge, fear or uncertainty. Her heart was never touched by stirrings of hate, nor did it ever melt with tenderness. Sometimes, when she saw good and evil pitted together in a struggle, she would bet on which of them would be successful. But she was indifferent as to whether vice or virtue triumphed as long as she won her gamble.

She had enjoyed the struggle between Solquest the zentyre and Elsie Constance, the ghostly child. When they struck a bargain in the concert hall and made promises to each other she had remained unmoved. It was no surprise to the Custodian that Solquest was preparing to avenge himself on Merrick Town.

She knew that he would break a promise, made in a moment of fear, as carelessly as he would snap a dry twig beneath his feet. He was unworthy of her attention—and would not have attracted it but for the challenge he uttered. It made her pause in flight and listen.

"Come gamble with me, bird," coaxed the zentyre. "I have a gamble that you will enjoy but will not win. Come to my island and play games, bird. Or are you a coward who fears to gamble with the great zentyre?"

Day after day she heard his voice, low and bewitching as he repeated his taunts.

"I will ignore him," she insisted to herself. But her blood was beginning to race. Why did he wish to risk gambling with the Custodian of the Dark Rill? She would defeat him, destroy him, humiliate him. Finally she was no longer able to resist the lure in his voice and she left the safety of the Dark Rill.

A pink glow lit the mist surrounding Isealina. Solquest watched as the colour deepened until it looked like a cloud catching the last red flames of the setting sun. The murmuring growl from the luvenders rose in a swell of excitement as a bird appeared through the mist and rested upon a rock.

"Greetings, Custodian of the Dark Rill," said Solquest. "I once had the pleasure of visiting your home. Now I extend the same welcome to you."

The eyes of the bird were round and white. There was no warmth in them as she gazed around the island. She fluttered her wide, red-feathered wings and arched her neck towards Solquest. "You have been unable to rest easy, zentyre, since your return to Isealina. Now you call me to your island home with talk of a great gamble that will decide our destinies. That is the only reason I am here, zentyre. I want to gamble on your destruction."

Prologue

The luvenders spat. Saliva flew through the air, droplets of poison that evaporated when the white eyes of the bird gazed upon these creatures of evil. Her musical chuckle rang out as the luvenders scurried across the pebbled beach, long nails ready to claw the feathers from her body.

"Be at peace, luvenders," growled Solquest. "The Custodian of the Dark Rill may speak heedless words. But she is our guest. She has come to gamble with us." He bowed to the bird. "But first let us set the mood. Seven days of games—and then the final gamble. You wish to gamble on my destruction? So be it. I will gamble that only one of us, either the great Solquest or the Custodian of the Dark Rill, can enjoy the power of eternal life. If you lose you will forfeit your journey through eternity. If I lose I too will disappear from Isealina, forever."

The Custodian shivered as if she had flown too close to the edge of a flame. "Let the gambling begin," she sang.

For seven days Solquest and the Custodian gambled on many things, the fall of a dice, or the height of waves dashing against the rocks of Isealina. They guessed the number of raindrops in a wind-swept shower, and how many insects crawled within the crevices of the mulchantus garden. The luvenders raced upon the pebbled shore, faster than the speed of light, and vast bets were laid upon the winner. By the end of seven days the bird was crazed with gambling fever. It ran like a fire through her blood.

"More! More!" she cried. "Let the gamble of destiny commence." She was strong and free as the air. No one had the power to surpass her.

"As you say—let the gamble of destiny commence," growled Solquest. "I bet you your life that you cannot enter the tribab or see the secrets that lie within my home."

The bird glided low over the mist-covered dome. "Foolish zentyre. If I were to use the full might of my magic I could move inside your tribab as easily as a stone falls through water."

"Boastful words. Nothing more," smirked Solquest. "Will you utter them with such confidence when you have strayed forever from the path of eternity?" The Custodian of the Dark Rill tilted her head in proud defiance. "Let us gamble then, zentyre. I will wager my life against your destruction and I will sing high notes of triumph from within your tribab."

"Done!" roared the zentyre. "In three days'

Prologue

time one of us will declare victory."

Luvenders danced upon the shore and uttered hiccupping cries of glee. They felt no sense of fear as they stared at the Custodian.

"Done!" she cried. "This mist is as fragile as a cobweb resting on the dew of early morning." Her white eyes widened in concentration as she tried to see beyond the shimmering haze that embraced the tribab. She closed her eyes and willed herself inside the enchanted home of Solquest. But her claws just sank into drifting waves of silvery cloud. Her voice rose above the mist, high, sweet notes of command, and when the black flowering rows of mulchantus swayed in rhythm, it seemed as if the ledges were alive with her music.

Singing increased her magical powers but at the end of her song the entrance to the tribab still remained hidden beneath the mist. Again she sang and sang as if she would split the tribab apart. By evening time she knew that she had failed but still, in the grip of gambling fever, she continued to sing throughout the night. When dawn split the horizon her voice was growing husky. Those who listened wondered if her heart would burst from the effort of creating such sound.

"Admit that you are defeated, Custodian,"

Solquest's cry of triumph rang out jubilantly from within the tribab.

She heard the harsh cackling laughter of the luvenders. Her voice rose again in song. All day she sang and through the following night, and the next day and the night that passed over Isealina, until her song was just a croaking whimper and the feathers began to fall from her wings.

"Eternity will only last for a few hours more," shrieked Solquest. "Never," whispered the bird and felt a trembling weariness sweep over her. "I must stop," she whispered. "I am weak and my magic fails me. I must return and renew my strength in the Dark Rill."

But she did not understand emotions of fear or loss. Only the need to win. The lure of the gamble controlled her. On and on she sang, the notes falling flat and tuneless over the island. Then, just as time was running out for the Custodian of the Dark Rill, the mist disappeared. An entrance appeared in the tribab, revealing a narrow passageway. The bird stopped singing.

"I have won," she thought; but she was too weary to feel the normal surge of excitement that came over her when she was successful. Her wings flapped weakly as she spread them

Prologue

in a wide span and swooped towards the passageway. She could hear the luvenders screaming.

"We will be destroyed, Master. The Custodian plans your destruction. How will we survive without you?"

"I have lost everything," cried Solquest.

The eyes of the bird darted nervously about. She heard the zentyre's cry of terror. It reverberated through the tribab but there was something...something...The bird was too weak to ponder, too weak to heed the uneasy beat of her heart as she entered the enchanted home of the zentyre.

She was in a cavern, high and deep, with rocky steps leading downwards. A shaft of sunshine came through a concealed opening. The walls were yellow-streaked and damp; stalactites hung like ghostly tentacles from the ceiling. Some were thick as tree trunks, tapering into a point; others as fine as the finest sewing needle—and as sharp. Distorted and hunched shapes crouched on the ground, staring at her from baleful eyes. Suddenly they moved and the bird shuddered as she realised that they were luvenders, crawling over the stone-flagged floor. She looked around but there was no sign of Solquest. Then his voice rang out.

"Foolish bird, filled with the mad arrogance of a gambler. I knew that this vice would destroy you. And I spoke words of truth."

The Custodian of the Dark Rill swooped around the vast cavern, frantically searching for an escape through the passageway. But it had disappeared. She could not summon the strength to gather her magical power around her.

"You have exhausted your power," gloated the zentyre. "Did you really think you could penetrate the home of Solquest? Foolish bird. Once my tribab was protected by the crystals of Ulum, nothing could enter it. In your lust to win your gamble you have destroyed yourself."

Desperately the bird tried to find the direction of Solquest's voice. It came from behind a long thin stalactite that hung from the centre of the dome. "Why do you look so fearful, Custodian? Your heart is like a rock that has never known the scratch of an insect, or the bite of moss on its surface. Has it now learned what it is like to suffer? To be humiliated? Is it to know sorrow and regret before it stops beating? And pain? What do you know of pain, foolish bird? It will be my pleasure to teach you this final lesson."

Suddenly a stalactite broke loose with a loud snap and flew towards her, its point aimed directly at her heart.

"This stake of evil can kill the Custodian of the Dark Rill and end her reign of eternity." Solquest stood on the floor of the tribab, his face twisted in a mask of joy as the stalactite pierced the red-feathered chest of the bird. Blood dripped upon the floor of the tribab. The passageway once more opened.

"Your journey through the Dark Rill of eternity is at an end," gloated Solquest as he watched the bird twist in agony.

"Let me die now, this instant," she wept. "I cannot live with this pain for one second longer. I beg you, zentyre. Release me from it."

"Suffer, Custodian! You will not be able to remove the spear of Solquest from your heart until I decide that the time is ripe for your death. In the moment that I bring destruction upon the town of Merrick your miserable existence will end. Be gone, Custodian. Fly across the waves. Spill your blood upon the sea. Solquest has won his gamble. Solquest has been avenged."

1
Visions from Isealina

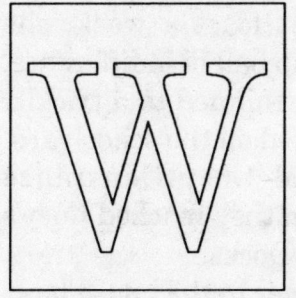hen the bell for the end of class rang throughout Merrick Comprehensive, the pupils flung themselves out of the school gates with the energy of a waterfall suddenly released from captivity. It was Friday evening, the beginning of the October mid-term break. Free! Free! Free! The word danced on every tongue as girls and boys poured, flowed, cascaded, leapt and raced along School Yard Parade.

The sound of approaching footsteps caused sweet-shop owners and bus drivers to breathe deeply and brace themselves for twenty minutes of bedlam. The thunder of jubilant voices scattered pigeons and sent the school janitor's cat streaking to the safety of the bicycle shed roof where she snarled and spat in temper. She was a cat who liked to doze in peace and resented this invasion of her space, an ordeal she was forced to endure five days a week. But today's level of noise had a holiday ring to it so, with the knowledge that she would doze uninterrupted for at least a week, she settled herself into a plump ball of indifference. The waterfall slowed and thinned to a trickle. Silence once more descended on the schoolyard.

Paula Masterson and Lucy Constance paused for a moment when they reached Lucy's turn-off point at Merrick Docks.

"Won't you bring him over to the house later on?" Paula asked. "We're dying to meet him. He sounds brilliant!"

"Oh! He is," replied Lucy, making scrumptious noises and rolling her eyes, appreciatively. Lucy lived with her mother, Kate, in the small gate-lodge in the shadow of Merrick Heights. Kate ran the GRUB BUG company—a mobile take-away van painted in the image of a garishly-coloured bug. It had become a popular and familiar sight along the docks and in the town centre since the Constance family moved from Lepping Vale to their new home in Merrick over four months ago.

On reaching the gate-lodge she discovered that Jon Freeman had already arrived. He was

Visions from Isealina 3

taller than she remembered and even better-looking than she had imagined. All she had forgotten about was his personality. When she lived in Lepping Vale, she had fancied Jon Freeman. But then so had all her friends. It was a collective infatuation and none of them actually knew him. Just to worship him from a distance was sufficient. Tall and slim, with dark hair falling over his eyes, he was as broodingly handsome as a pop star. Apart from being the son of wealthy parents and Lepping Vale's most successful athlete, he was a brilliant student without (and this was the most sickening part of all) having to make any effort to study.

His clothes were cool, designer-branded right down to his underpants, or so he claimed. As if fortune had not already smiled enough on him, he also travelled around the world with his parents to the most exotic holiday spots.

Unfortunately his mother, Pearl, had discovered that a son, taller than herself and with the beginnings of designer-stubble on his chin, was an uncomfortable indicator that she was not as young as she liked to pretend. So, during the October mid-term school break, she had departed to a sun-soaked hot-spot in the Caribbean and so Jon had been dispatched to stay with her good friend, Kate Constance, for a week, to learn something about what his glamorous mother called "the less privileged side of life."

Jon's visit taught Lucy an important lesson —that often it was better, far better, to worship from afar. Finding out what a person was really like on a one-to-one basis could be very disillusioning. She blushed with embarrassment to think she had once belonged to a secret group known as Freeman's Fanciers, consoling herself with the fact that she had only been twelve years old at the time. The horrible thing was that Jon appeared to know about her infatuation and kept putting his arms around her in a most possessive way. Whenever she told him to "get lost" he flashed his know-it-all smile at her, paying no attention to her protests.

By the time he returned home at the end of the mid-term break Lucy's friends breathed a sigh of relief.

"If that's what her friends in Lepping Vale were like, no wonder she's so happy since she moved," said Sally Masterson in a tone of voice that expressed the superior quality of young people from Merrick Town.

Initially Valerie Collins thought Jon was

Visions from Isealina

terrific and listened willingly when he told her about his straight A grades in all honour subjects and how he always scored the winning try for his rugby team. But it did not take her long to discover that Jon had a habit of interrupting her every time she managed to get a word in edgeways about herself and her own interests, or else he yawned and looked blankly over her shoulder.

"A self-opinionated dork," she told the Masterson sisters, who nodded vigorously. Paula had allowed Jon Freeman to read her poetry and watched furiously as he corrected two spelling mistakes, declared that her poems were badly formed, immature and—after reading the zentyre collection—"somewhat more than risible."

"Wow!" gasped Sally. "Now tell her what you *hate* about them!"

Paula thumped her sister on the shoulder and stormed off to her bedroom to check the dictionary and cry for two hours when she discovered that the word "risible" meant "ludicrous."

On the fourth day of his stay with the Constance family Lucy brought him to Lower Merrick Green to see Alan Bradshaw's laboratory. This was a large wooden shed, built by

Alan's long-suffering parents in an effort to prevent him blowing up their home.

"Alan, this is Jon," Lucy introduced the two boys.

"Jon—spelled without an H," said Jon, as if this omission was vitally important. He had no intention of going through life with a name as common as "John."

The two boys stared at each other with mutual hostility.

"What exactly is this quaint little hidey-hole?" asked Jon, glancing around Alan's laboratory with a quizzical expression. Everything about Merrick Town was "quaint", according to Jon, who always spoke with a drawling, high-pitched accent. On this occasion his tone suggested that he had strayed into a child's play-house by mistake. Alan's newest invention, disrespectfully nick-named "Bodwin's Battler" by his friends, amused Jon enormously. "What's it supposed to be?" he asked.

Alan was embarrassed, and annoyed with Lucy Constance for bringing him over. "I'm inventing a machine to pick up evidence of the supernatural," he muttered. "It's based on a design I found in a book that was written a long time ago by Professor B K Bodwin."

"Oh wow!" said Jon. "How quaint! Science and the supernatural. An interesting combination. What will you do for an encore? Brew the hearts of toads over a bunsen burner?"

"Oh mortification!" moaned Lucy.

Although his visit only lasted for a week this was, as far as Robert Collins was concerned, seven days too long.

"He's jealous," his sister, Valerie, confided in Lucy when the two girls were working in the cookhouse. "He's nicknamed him the H-less Wimp because he thinks you fancy him."

Lucy was delighted with this piece of information. "I used to fancy him. But I was only a child then," she admitted with the superior wisdom of a fourteen-year-old. "Now I think he's a real face-pain. Tell Robert he's got nothing to worry about."

"I will like glue," said Valerie, with sisterly unconcern. "Let him stew."

And stew he did. Robert, who rather liked Lucy Constance, had discovered a streak of jealousy within himself that was strong enough to make him want to re-shape the perfect contours of Jon Freeman's nose every time he saw him casually draping his arm around Lucy's shoulders.

On the last evening of Jon's visit the staff of

the cookhouse were busily preparing food for the night time GRUB BUG run. Kate and Old Knees-Up were due back soon from the town centre where they had been working for the afternoon. They would expect everything to be ready, and the cookhouse manager, Mrs Shine—who was no respecter of straight A grades or amazing rugby records—had bullied Jon into helping out.

"Seeing as how you've nothing better to do than admire yourself, you might as well give us a hand to get the evening supplies ready," she said, discovering him pouting at his reflection in the cookhouse mirror. "Go on. Just look around and you'll find loads to do." She shooed him away with her hands. When she opened the oven door delicious cake smells wafted on hot air through the cookhouse.

Lucy busied herself washing pots and pans. Valerie made coleslaw and potato salad, her unruly red hair tied up in a white cap. On Friday nights and Saturdays she worked for the GRUB BUG Company. Jon, after a quick look around the cookhouse, began sketching out a plan that would organise their work much more effectively.

"Well! Shoot me in the foot!" declared Mrs Shine, glancing at his drawing. "What a clever genius we have in our midst. Listen, Mister Bird-brain, for the moment it's physical rather than mental assistance that I need—so how about kissing those potatoes with a knife."

He sighed, giving Lucy a meaningful smile that suggested there were other things he would prefer to kiss. But Lucy was paying him no attention. Instead she clutched the side of the table on which she had started slicing onions and tried to remain calm as the floor tilted beneath her feet. For an instant she seemed to lose her balance and had the sensation that everything familiar was drawing away from her. This was not a new experience. It had happened on a number of occasions since the night of the mud-slide.

On that occasion, in the middle of the Cold Command Charlie concert, a sizeable portion of Merrick Heights had been eroded during a heavy rain-storm. The mud had flowed down the side of the Heights and, although all the young fans attending the concert had escaped the mud-flow, it had destroyed the concert hall. Lucy did not miss the the neon-flashing, gaudy building or the bleak old mill that originally stood on the site. But there were times when she bitterly resented the powers that Elsie Constance, the ghostly child, had passed on to her before she disappeared on that mysterious night, a month ago.

Since then, Lucy's moods had veered between fear of the unknown and a sense of courageous excitement that she had been chosen for some grand, mysterious mission.

Her fear surfaced whenever she remembered the final words Elsie Constance had uttered. "Do not grieve for me. I will be at peace." The ghostly child had put her hands on Lucy's shoulders. "But you must not trust the word of Solquest. When he returns to Isealina he will be able to draw on deep magic that will bring him back to Merrick Town. And I will not be here to protect you. You must prevent that happening. You already have courage. Now I leave you my strength and my wisdom."

But she had said nothing about strange images that would sweep across Lucy's mind, filling her head with colour and sound, so that she did not know if it was her imagination running riot or part of the legacy inherited from the ghostly child. Before those images flashed into her mind the ground seemed to sway for a few seconds and she felt a nauseous dizzy sensation.

When it passed she saw pictures, the island of Isealina and the luvenders scurrying along

Visions from Isealina

flowering ledges towards an enormous dome. Sometimes she could see into the dome where the luvenders slept in a warren of tunnels and caves that led from the central cavern. This cavern was dominated by a grim-looking slab of rock upon which a glass orb rested. She did not know what lay within the round ball of smoke-streaked glass, yet each time she saw it she began to tremble.

Then just as suddenly as they appeared the pictures faded and she was left with the bewildered feeling that she had snapped out of a nightmare.

"Lucy, if those onions are making you cry so much go outside and get some air." Mrs Shine's voice interrupted Lucy's concentration.

"No, no. I want to stay..." But her sentence trailed away. The floor had steadied beneath her feet but the urge to run towards the old site of the mill was overwhelming. The site had been exposed after the removal of all the rubble and only one low wall remained standing. As if pulled along on an invisible thread, she walked slowly out of the cookhouse and along the cobbled path. She remembered another time when her footsteps had dragged along the same path; red eyes in the night; a voice beckoning her towards the old mill that had been lit by a shimmering mist.

"I won't think about it. I won't! I won't!" But she knew that the evil of Solquest still lingered above the mill site. She touched the battered piece of iron shaped in a heart that she wore around her neck since Robert had given it to her on her fourteenth birthday. As always, it helped to steady her thoughts.

Her feet moved over the uneven cement slabs towards the wall. She thought she would fall and held onto it to steady herself, uttering a breathless whimper of fear as she waited for the pictures to appear.

In the beginning the visions had been filled with such noise and confusion that she had clamped her hands over her ears. But that made her even more confused and afterwards her head ached with a dull pain. Then she had learned to stay calm, to allow her mind to become a pool; deep and silent, not even a ripple disturbing the surface, not even a stone falling, falling through this bottomless void. She was able to listen to the noise when it came; to allow the colours to unfold until they formed pictures and she could make sense from chaos.

Lucy tensed as the pictures began to take shape. She was standing outside the dome that rose above the island of Isealina. A thick mist swirled around it but that did not matter to Lucy, who could see inside the dome, where a red cloud exploded and trailed across her mind like a falling star.

"Be calm and listen and watch," she told herself. When she heard a cry, an agonised cry of pain that came from a living thing, she wondered how long the creature could survive before being silenced forever. Despite the terror of the sound there was music in the strange cry, wounded notes that wept and begged for mercy.

She stayed quiet and the red cloud began to shape itself into the twisted body of a bird. A red-feathered bird with blank, white eyes, desperately fluttering her wings as she tried to stay in the air. Lucy saw, deep in the heart of the bird, a sliver of ice; no, not ice, something even more deadly and sharper than the beak of the bird, sharper than the wind as it penetrates the invisible crevice of a stone.

With a final, desperate flutter of wings, the bird rose in the air. It flew through a narrow passageway and out into the forest of black-headed flowers, over the banks of a river where green stones gleamed beneath the water. Red feathers scattered in the wind as the bird swooped sickeningly, almost crashing into the rocks. But somehow she managed to find the strength to rise and disappear into the mist.

Lucy held tightly to the wall. Every muscle in her body ached and her breath tried to release itself in a scream. But she knew that somewhere in the stillness of her mind she had the courage to control her fear.

"I'm going to ignore you," she whispered. "In a moment you will fade from my mind and I will never see you again."

"Yes, you will. You will see me forever in your dreams." Lucy read this message clearly in those lost white eyes. The vision began to fade and disappear into another dimension that had been revealed to Lucy by Elsie Constance. She stood in the shelter of the wall for a long time, hearing her breath returning to normal, feeling calm again as the trembling stopped.

2
The First Quarrel

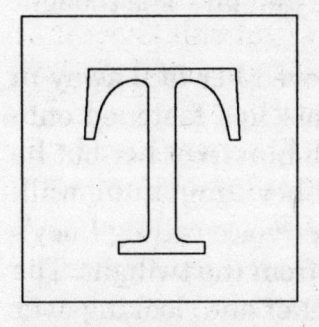

Twilight was deepening into a haze of indigo cloud. The sound of the GRUB BUG horn blasted the silence of the river road. Lights shone from the window of the cookhouse. It was cold on the site of the old mill. Fingers clamped across her eyes. Someone's breath was warm on her neck.

"Hey Lucy, guess who?" She was spun around, the fingers released. Jon Freeman was standing in front of her. He moved closer, putting his arms around her shoulders. "I knew you were waiting here for me. But that old bat kept dumping potatoes on me. Talk about youth exploitation." He was smiling and confident as he tilted her chin and looked into her eyes. "Onion tears. That was a neat way of getting out of the cookhouse. And here's your reward."

Before she realised what he was doing he bent his head and kissed her. His mouth was open, his lips taut and dry.

"Ugh! It's like kissing a jam-jar," she thought in disgust.

"Buzz off, Jon," she moved her face away in a jerky movement and his lips fastened onto her ear. She tried to push him from her but he only laughed and pinned her against the wall.

Then there was another voice calling Lucy's name, a figure emerging from the twilight. The voice was a gasp of disbelief and, looking over Jon's shoulder, Lucy was just in time to see the back view of Robert Collins's denim jacket as he strode purposefully along the cobbled path, away from her and back to the cookhouse. She had the feeling that he wanted to dash away from what he had seen but his stride remained steady. He was soon swallowed by the gathering darkness.

Lucy did not talk much about Robert, or how she felt about him, to anyone. But to herself she hugged each encounter they had, the flickering sensation in her stomach when she caught him staring at her, their eyes asking questions, until one of them looked away in embarrassment. It was delightful and exciting

The First Quarrel

and very, very private—until Jon Freeman destroyed it.

"He must have travelled out from town in the GRUB BUG," she said to Jon. "*Now* what's he going to think?"

"Stupid cretin," replied Jon, not at all disturbed by the interruption. "Don't pay any attention to him." He blocked her way when she tried to move around him.

"Get your stupid hands off me at once!" Lucy reached out and dealt Jon a stinging and very satisfying blow across his cheek. He staggered back, his eyes narrowing in disbelief. "What's that for? Are you playing hard to get or something stupid like that?"

"No! No! No! I just wish you'd get it through your thick head that I'm not interested in you!"

"Listen to the protests of Lucy Constance! The number one paid-up member of Freeman's Fanciers." His condescending tone sent the colour racing across her cheeks. How could he know about that?

Kate always said that a mistake faced is a mistake erased—so Lucy tossed her head and glared defiantly back at him. "We all make mistakes, Jon Freeman. And that was my biggest one. But, just for your record of achievements, let me tell you that in the kissing grades you score E minus!" And then, afraid that he might manage to get in the last word, she left him holding the side of his glowing face and ran back to the cookhouse.

"Where's Robert?" she asked the others.

"Oh, you're a great little Miss Dosser," said Mrs Shine, fluttering about like an angry pigeon. "You come here at once and finish those onions."

"In a minute, Mrs Shine," Lucy yelled and ran out through Colin's Gates. Down by the river she found Robert leaning over the wall, intently watching the flow of the water.

"Why did you go off like that?"

"Like what?" He shrugged off the hand she laid on his arm.

"You could have waited and let me explain."

"What have you got to explain? We don't own each other or anything stupid like that!" He picked up a stone and skimmed it across the water. It hopped neatly, like a child playing hopscotch, and disappeared into the centre of the river.

"Then why are you so mad?"

"Mad! I'm not mad. I'm just standing here minding my own business and you come along and start bothering me!"

"I didn't want that creep to kiss me. It was

The First Quarrel

pure yuck if you want to know."

"Oh sure! That's not what it looked like from where I was standing." Another stone was skimmed with fierce concentration. It fell flat and disappeared under the ripples. "Now look at what you've made me do!" He sounded extremely irritated that she should come along and distract him from skimming stones and glowering at the sleepy seagulls who swooped lazily over the river walls.

"Sor-ryyyyyyyyy!" snapped Lucy. Suddenly she realised that she wanted a row. She wanted to scream long and loudly across the smoothly-flowing water, to disturb the apparent serenity of the evening shadows as they gathered around her and hid the menace of the old mill site. She wanted to stamp her feet and lash out at anything, even Robert Collins, if it would quell the fear that was growing inside her, the knowledge that the island of Isealina was drawing her nearer with each vision.

"There's nothing to be sorry about. Do you think I care who you kiss? Huh! I've more important things to do with my time. The two of you looked so stupid!!" Robert sounded scornful, turning his back on her to look towards Tobin Bridge and beyond, where the distant lights of Merrick Town lit the sky with a bonfire hue.

"Oh yeah! Then why are you sulking like a big stupid baby who's lost his soother?"

"Who's sulking? I'm laughing or haven't you noticed? Ha! Ha! Ha! Haaaaa!"

From then on the conversation was downhill all the way. By the time it ended, Robert knew that he was a macho pig and a jealous, toe-ragged dork. Faced with such stridency he was awed into silence but, gathering his resources, he told her that she was a selfish two-timing flirt and that her behaviour would make anyone else—except him—as sick as a parrot.

Lucy could never remember feeling so angry. But there was also a most disconcerting urge to giggle at the stupidity of their behaviour. "We're having our first row," she thought. "And Valerie's right. He *is* jealous." The realisation made her feel quite giddy and smug. But *that* could wait until later. In the meantime they glared and out-stared each other from eyes that darkened like storm-clouds as they tried to think of suitable insults. Colour mounted in their cheeks.

They told lies about hating each other and not caring if they never saw each other, ever again. Then when they were totally convinced that there was nothing left in their friendship

The First Quarrel

and that they would walk on the opposite sides of the road if they chanced to meet—even if one side happened to be under water—the anger exhausted itself like a squall of wind that suddenly dies in the aftermath of a storm.

Robert's eyes seemed huge in the glare of the overhanging river lamps, deep brown and full of misery, unable to figure a way of bringing their argument to an end. Wordlessly they moved together, suddenly wondering why on earth they had been fighting. Lucy kissed him, blotting out the memory of Jon Freeman's bullying behaviour, and even the memory of Isealina began to fade. Robert made a muffled sound of relief and pulled her close against him.

"I'm really sorry for going on like that," he apologised, when they drew apart. "You said I was jealous and you're right. But it wasn't really you and Jon together that made me mad. It's something else...something that I can't understand...but it has to do with Elsie Constance. It's as if she's taken away a part of you that I can't get close to any more." He did not have the words to tell her that wherever she went, even if it was only into her mind, he wanted to be close beside her.

He traced his finger over the full curve of her lower lip. It felt soft and warm beneath his touch.

Suddenly Lucy wanted to tell him everything. But should she? Would it frighten him? Maybe he would think she was crazy. Hallucinating or something weird like that. As always her shyness and the need to be the same as her friends won out and she hesitated.

Lucy knew that the strange things that had happened during the rock concert, and the mud-flow that had almost killed the fans, were only hazy memories of evil in the dreams of her friends. The day after the mud-flow they had written down the details of Solquest's confrontation with Elsie Constance. But even as they wrote they could feel their thoughts wandering and it had been extremely difficult to concentrate on the words that jumbled together as they wrote. But they had succeeded in entering their recollections in Robert's journal. Unlike them Lucy did not need to read the journal to remember. Her links with Elsie Constance kept the memory of the zentyre and his luvenders vividly locked in her mind.

Then when the mysterious pictures came, they set her apart from her friends, made her feel different, weird and off-the-wall. So she hugged the secrets of Isealina to herself and when her friends looked anxiously at her and

The First Quarrel

asked if something was upsetting her, she brushed off their enquiries with an airy toss of her head. Sometimes she felt that she was the only person to inhabit two worlds—the ordinary one, and a mind world of crazy images. It made her feel very lonely.

Robert was looking at her so intently that the words bubbled to her lips but instead she began to talk about Jon Freeman and found herself admitting to the shame of once being a Freeman's Fancier. She giggled with embarrassment and he hooted with laughter and everything was fun again—except that she knew she was talking about Jon Freeman because it stopped her pouring out her fears of crazy mind-pictures and the feeling of being a witness to events unfolding in that mysterious island of evil.

They were interrupted by Kate's voice, sounding impatient as it drifted along the river road. It was followed by a loud tootling from the horn of the GRUB BUG.

"Mrs Shine will peel me like an onion when she gets her hands on me," moaned Lucy. "We'd better go."

Everyone except Jon was watching them as they walked nonchalantly into the cookhouse. Lucy endured a tirade of abuse from Mrs Shine and sly grins from Valerie. No matter how hard she tried she was unable to wipe the smile from her face as Robert began to help her slice a mountain of onions. If all rows could end like that it might be worth having one every week. The following day Jon Freeman returned to Lepping Vale and everyone was quite happy to forget about him until the Christmas holidays.

3
The Start of the Christmas Holidays

Merrick 200 became the buzz word as the pupils of Merrick Comprehensive began their Christmas holidays. Two hundred years before, on New Year's Eve, the first ship sailed up South Dock and officially opened the port of Merrick. It had fired a gun salute to celebrate a new beginning—and a new year. This ship, called *Triumph*, had been renovated and was a museum piece on the South Dock, a tourist attraction and a regular feature on school tours. On this New Year's Eve it would once again sail up the river to the sound of cheers and the bells of Merrick Cathedral. Weather permitting, a brilliant display of fireworks would be set off from the deck of *Triumph* as well as a laser display that would light the sky for miles around. To add to the carnival atmosphere, everyone was being encouraged to wear fancy dress.

But before this major event happened there would be other things to enjoy—Christmas parties to attend, the Brains of Merrick team competition that would take place on 30 December, and the youth-club discos. There was a lot to celebrate and school scarves were waved as flags of freedom when the pupils emerged from the narrow confines of School Yard Parade.

Paula was sandwiched between four identical blonde boys, collectively known as the Quados. They were the bane of her life. Paula the poet, quiet and pensive, with words running like a fever through her mind, had once dropped her standards and under pressure from the boys, who had formed a rock group, written a song for them called "Marmalade Madness." She still shuddered every time she remembered it. Sometimes when she had the blues and her confidence was at zero point zero she wondered if "Marmalade Madness" would survive forever to haunt her—and the generations that followed her—while her wonderful poetry perished in the passage of time.

Sally, Valerie, Alan, Robert and Lucy walked together. Robert kept glancing at Lucy and

The Start of the Christmas Holidays

looking away again before she noticed. She was close beside him yet she could have been a hundred miles away. Her cheekbones seemed more prominent than usual and there were dark shadows smudging the skin beneath her eyes.

"Is anything wrong?" he asked.

"No. Not at all. Everything's fine," she replied in a bright, false voice and smiled at him. "Why do you ask?"

He shrugged. "I don't know. Just things." He was unable to put it into words; to describe the uneasiness that came from her, the sense that she was looking beyond him and the unruly crowd, to some private place where he could not follow.

Lucy shivered and moved closer to him. The images from Isealina had intensified over the last two weeks. So had her feelings of apprehension. There was a story in the pictures: the mist with the heart in its centre, the geography of the island that became clearer each time she saw it. On certain nights she heard the lonely cry of the red-feathered bird in her sleep. The cry seemed to be drawing closer to the gate-lodge, an ever-growing clamour of pain that always woke her with a jerking sensation of falling from a great height and she would lie, staring into the darkness, wondering if it had been a dream-sound or a warning that she could not yet understand.

Sensing Robert's concern, Lucy forced herself to think of other things and join in the excitement around her. Gradually the crowd was dispersing. The Quados, having tried in vain to persuade Paula to come with them, entered The Goldfish Bowl to buy fish and chips. She joined the others who had stopped outside Cassie's Video Market. They had made arrangements to watch a video in Alan's house. Pocket money was pooled and the usual argument began as to which video should be taken out. Because nobody could agree Alan decided that they should go for *The Screaming Coffins* once again. Admittedly it would be their third time to watch it. But as it had a verdict of "brilliant" it saved arguing in the rain.

The misty drizzle was growing stronger by the time they reached Alan's house. Spacer, the Bradshaws' large black dog, flung himself upon them in a wet frenzy of welcome. Alan's parents had not arrived home from work and his grandfather was out driving the GRUB BUG. Alan offered to make them dinner and busied himself in the kitchen. Much to Valerie's disgust this turned out to be popcorn,

The Start of the Christmas Holidays

mountains of it, biscuits and orange juice.

"Oh wow! Cuisine a la Disgusting. It *really* breaks me up to see you going to so much trouble," she mocked. "Are you sure you wouldn't like to lie down for an hour after all that hard work?"

"That's gratitude for you." He appealed for sympathy from the others but they were too busy dipping their hands into the popcorn bowl.

Lucy noticed a copy of Professor B K Bodwin's *Zentyre Magic—Illusion or Reality?* on a book shelf. Alan had discovered the book in a book-barrow at an open-air market. The findings in the professor's book were vague but they added weight to their belief that there were others who also believed in the force of zentyre evil. Alan was convinced that he could build a sound machine that would defeat the chant of the zentyre, based on the diagrams in the book.

"Think of something else!" Lucy ordered herself and dipped her hand into the popcorn bowl. The rain and the wind tapping wet branches against the Bradshaws' lounge window, did nothing to dampen the enthusiasm of her friends. They simply assumed that, starting the following morning, the sun, however wintry, would appear on cue for the entire holiday.

Sprawling in positions that were designed to ruin their postures for the rest of their lives, they watched *The Screaming Coffins*. Sally, showing off, dangled her legs across the back of an armchair and, with her head hanging down, watched the film from an upside-down angle. She claimed this added a more eerie dimension to it. The others did not remind her that she had huddled underneath the table with her head buried in a cushion the first time she watched it. She threw popcorn in the air and tried to catch it in her mouth. Mostly she was unsuccessful. Spacer, using his tongue like a mechanical shovel, trawled the floor, gobbling up all mis-aimed popcorn and thumping his tail in gratitude. Occasionally a slurping sound disturbed the sound-track of *The Screaming Coffins* as straws poked the bottom of orange juice cartons and sucked fresh air.

"Is everything all right in the piggery?" asked Mrs Bradshaw, who had just arrived in from work. They grunted an affirmative, unable to move their eyes from the screen where a beautiful vampire with blooded lips and claw-like fingers beckoned her victim closer, closer, ever closer to the edge of her coffin. Mrs Bradshaw, having coped with one hour of peak-time traffic, decided that her

The Start of the Christmas Holidays

nerves would be unable to stand the strain of *The Screaming Coffins* and opted for the serenity of the kitchen. Her retreat went unnoticed. The camera zoomed into the vampire's green eyes, wild and terrible, as they bewitched the hero who was preparing to jump into her open coffin.

"Her eyes are just like yours, Lucy," chirped Sally.

This sudden comment caused everyone to jump, and Lucy to shriek with indignation. "Nuts to you, Sally Masterson. They are not!"

"Belt up!" ordered Alan. "This is the really good bit."

They watched in fascinated horror as the vampire's teeth sank into her victim's neck.

"That's really disgusting!" Sally gasped, quickly rearranging her body into a normal viewing position as the vampire began her evening meal.

"Yuck!" said Paula. "I'm going to become a vegetarian!" She burrowed deeper into the beanbag.

"Call that action! Valerie could give her lessons any day," declared Alan. He took cover behind a cushion as the love of his life, teeth bared, dived upon him.

"You want action, baby? I'll give it to you,"

she growled and the two of them were off, wrestling with each other on a baggy old armchair as Valerie tried to sink her teeth into his willing neck.

"Boring! Boring!" chorused the other four. They tried to ignore them, stuffed their mouths with biscuits and turned up the volume.

Lucy could feel Robert's shoulder resting against her arm. They were sharing a sofa with Spacer who, sick of pop-corn, had tried to slink in between them. Robert's knee had grimly resisted the dog's efforts to dislodge him from Lucy's side. Spacer had been forced to sit on her other side, which he did, ungraciously, snuggling down on the soft cushions and laying his huge black head on her lap.

"Some dogs have all the luck," Robert whispered. Casually she allowed her hand to slide from her lap. Her fingers curled in an invitation then, as the music swooped and the vampire fed, their hands were clasped tightly together.

Then suddenly it happened again. The room faded. Even the mad vampire disappeared into a silver dot on the television screen. Robert's hand lost its warmth, grew cold and then withdrew, as everything else around her moved further and further away.

The Start of the Christmas Holidays

Lucy saw the image of Solquest standing at the entrance to a high, moss-covered dome. He held a glass orb in his hand. When it opened both sides rested in the palms of his hands and a mist began to escape, slowly spreading outwards like smoke from a chimney until it formed a shimmering cloud in front of him. Lucy looked into the mist and saw a heart, listened to the beat...beat...beating rhythm. She held her breath and waited. The mist became stronger, more condensed. It tightened around the heart so that the beat slowed, an unsteady, fluttering sound as if it was in pain.

Then she heard a voice and recognised the grating sound of Solquest's chant.

> *Great is the power*
> *That will be released*
> *By the crystals of Ulum.*
> *Strong is the vengeance*
> *That will be unleashed*
> *By the zentyre, Solquest.*
> *Sad is the heart*
> *When its life has ceased*
> *To beat in Merrick Town.*

"Keep beating...keep beating...please!" whispered Lucy, not understanding what the image meant but knowing that the mist intended to destroy the heart. Then there was nothing to see but the dense cloud and the throbbing heartbeat at last fell silent.

"Lucy! Can you hear me, Lucy?"

When she opened her eyes she was slumped against Robert's shoulder. Valerie held her hands and Paula was speaking softly to her, calling her name, calling her back to the warmth of the lounge. The television set had been turned off, the curtains drawn and the long-stemmed lamp had been switched on, the lamp-shade tilted so that the light was dim and her eyes were gradually able to adjust to it.

Lucy could see Spacer, his body pressed against the wall, whimpering sounds deep in his throat, his tail between his legs and his eyes, normally soft like melting butter, rolled upwards in white slits of fear.

"You must tell us what happened, Lucy... please tell...us!" Robert stopped, unable to continue.

Lucy cleared her throat. "I...I'm sorry!" She tried to stand up. There was no sensation in her feet and she fell back again, clinging to Valerie's hands.

Sally, the self-confessed coward of the group, gave a violent shudder. The others looked bewildered and terrified. They had been unable to believe it when Lucy closed her eyes and drifted away from them, losing consciousness as her face turned the colour of wax. That moment in time until her eyelids fluttered and opened had seemed like an eternity.

Without understanding anything they suspected that Lucy had journeyed into some other dimension where they could not follow her. But when the colour returned to Lucy's face she denied this, told them not to fuss and tiptoe around her as if she was a piece of glass. They admired her composure, yet worried nonetheless, a helpless, futile worrying that tried to protect her from something they could not touch, see, or even remember clearly except for distorted nightmares and sudden goose-pimply moments that made their hearts thud with suppressed fear.

Despite Lucy's reassurances that she had just suffered a moment of dizziness, Solquest was in all their thoughts. After their experience in the concert hall they had vowed to hold a zentyre meeting on a weekly basis. They would read from the notes they had made in the immediate aftermath of the mud-slide and plan the destruction of the zentyre. They uttered brave words and planned brave schemes but, somehow, every week, there was always an important excuse not to hold a meeting. Everyone pretended to be disappointed, not admitting to relief when yet another arrangement was cancelled. After a while the meetings slipped to the back of their minds. Nobody wanted to be the first to remember them.

"Tomorrow afternoon we'll have a meeting," declared Robert. "I think it's time we got together and pooled all our zentyre information. We haven't done that for ages."

This time there was real regret in Valerie's voice. "No can do," she said. "I'm working in the cookhouse. And so is Lucy."

"Then tomorrow night," said Robert and everyone nodded in agreement.

"I suppose Alan has fed the lot of you?" shouted Mrs Bradshaw.

"You could call it food if you had a problem with language," Valerie shouted back, trying to break the fear that lingered around them.

Alan did not appreciate her sense of humour. But it served its purpose and Mrs Bradshaw's voice calling from the kitchen had a reassuringly normal ring to it. "Then I suppose you wouldn't have any appetite left for pizzas followed by ice-cream and apple-tart?"

This foolish question brought the first sign

The Start of the Christmas Holidays

of life back to their faces.

"We might," yelled Sally. "We just might."

With one accord the friends rose. They were anxious to leave the lounge. The warm feeling of intimacy that was so evident between them when they were watching the film had disappeared and been replaced by a sense of uneasiness. For an instant they felt a sensation of chilly fingers stroking their faces. Imagination. Wild silly imaginings brought on by Lucy's weird behaviour. Each one of them held firmly to this thought. But they shivered as they felt the heat leave the room and wondered why the electric lamp, glowing in its shade, gave the impression that it was shining through a hazy cloud. When they blinked the impression had disappeared and, trying not to appear hurried, they headed out to the kitchen.

4
A Boy Called Rich

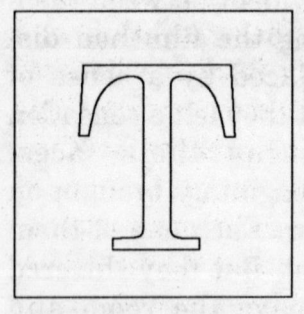

The cold symptoms of shock were passing, leaving in their place a nauseous sensation in the pit of Lucy's stomach. She toyed with her food, assuring Alan's mother that it was delicious but that she had no appetite.

"It *should* be delicious," agreed Mrs Bradshaw, pausing at the kitchen door on her way upstairs. "I bought it from the GRUB BUG on the way home from work. Kate tells me that she's thinking of opening a coffee shop when the concert hall gets underway."

Don Collins, the father of Valerie and Robert, had bought an old warehouse in East Dock on the opposite bank of the river. He hoped to convert it into a concert hall. Last week he had taken Kate out to dinner to

A Boy Called Rich

discuss his business venture with her. Lucy had woken at 2 a.m. and, hearing voices downstairs, had looked out of her bedroom window to see his car parked in front of the gate-lodge. Next morning, when Lucy asked her mother how the business meeting had gone, Kate looked vaguely into the distance and smiled. Lucy frowned, remembering this vagueness. It was so out of character for Kate, who normally buzzed with energy. She hoped her mother was not growing old and forgetful.

She was still thinking about her mother's strange behaviour when the telephone rang in the kitchen. Alan picked up the receiver, his face splitting into a wide grin. He placed his hand over the mouthpiece.

"Hey, you lot, it's Rich Harrison!"

"Rich!" whooped Sally. "Let me say hello to him."

"Wait a minute, wait a minute," said Alan, and uncovered the mouthpiece.

"Hey, Rich, the Masterson fan club of one sends her regards."

"And me," shouted Paula.

"Me too," shouted Valerie.

Sally grabbed the phone from Alan.

"Hey, Rich, it's me, Sally. How are you? When did they let you out of prison? Listen, I got this brilliant skateboard for my birthday and I'll bet you anything it'll leave your wheels standing still on Docker's Wharf. Your days are numbered, champ. Just wait till you see me in action."

"Who's that?" asked Mrs Bradshaw, returning to the kitchen.

"Rich!" they chorused.

"You must be joking!" she exclaimed. "I'm stony-broke and Christmas is only just around the corner."

"Oh Ma! It's Richard Harrison," said Alan, patiently.

"Oh Lord!" replied his mother. "Get out the sandbags—fast!"

"He's coming over tomorrow," yelled Sally. "His parents have come home from Nigeria for the Christmas holidays and he's just arrived from Leeside!"

"Tell him he's not doing wheelies in my house," ordered Mrs Bradshaw. "I had enough of his nonsense the last time he was home." There was a bellow of laughter from the other end of the line when this comment was relayed by Sally.

Lucy had only moved to Merrick Town in June and although she had heard about the legendary Rich from the others, she had not

A Boy Called Rich

yet met him. She knew that he was paralysed and that he tended to used his wheelchair as if he was taking part in a high-speed motor rally. He went to a boarding school called Leeside College and had flown out to join his parents in Nigeria for his summer holidays at the time when Lucy was moving to the gate-lodge.

Alan and Robert first met him at Merrick Athletics, the local sports club, where he had a keen interest in field and track athletics, winning the junior county javelin championship when he was fourteen.

Soon after that his parents, who ran a computer consultancy company, were offered a two-year contract in Nigeria and Rich was enrolled in Leeside College. He wrote to Alan regularly, claiming to hate the college and plotting ways of encouraging the principal to expel him. So far he had been unsuccessful, despite organising a protest against the college food and the amount of time Leeside pupils were forced to study.

Caught up in the momentary excitement that his name evoked, Lucy wondered what he would be like.

She found out the following morning. The rain had stopped but the mist lay low on the river as she ran towards Mrs Shine's house to collect the old woman's glasses. There were signs of development everywhere along Merrick Docks. Huge cranes jutted high above wooden hoardings surrounding half completed buildings. But despite the development of the docks there was still a lot of untouched waste ground. It provided ideal playing facilities for the young population of Merrick Town. In the summer time they used the river as a swimming pool. When the weather grew cold, the skateboard enthusiasts and the bikers turned their attention to Docker's Wharf, an alleyway that sloped downwards into a disused goods yard.

So it was that Lucy, taking a short cut through the goods yard with Mrs Shine's glasses in her hand, saw a human tornado in a wheelchair hurtling down the steep slopes, his hands raised in a victory salute while a screaming, wild-eyed Sally Masterson raced behind him on her skateboard.

"You must be Rich Harrison," Lucy said, as he braked just in time to avoid knocking her over.

"It's hard to mistake me," he grinned and shook her hand. "You must be Lucy with the pink hair. I've heard lots about you."

A Boy Called Rich

The pink streaks, the creation of Shiva, the female drummer with Cold Command Charlie, still tipped the very ends of Lucy's dark hair. She touched them self-consciously. "Me too...I mean I've heard lots about you." Listening to Sally's descriptions yesterday she had imagined that Rich Harrison would look like a blonde film star, while Robert had boasted so much about his athletic abilities that he had conjured up a Mr Muscle Man image.

Rich was neither of those things, just an ordinary boy in a check shirt, jeans and a quilted parka. His blonde hair was cut tight into his scalp and gave his face a gaunt appearance. But when he smiled his face lost its severity. Like every girl who had ever met him, Lucy envied the sweep of his eyelashes and his deep-blue eyes.

He was using a light-weight sport wheelchair and his broad-shouldered body seemed to be moulded into the seat. The back of it was covered in stickers and the seat had a battered, much-travelled look but Lucy noticed the well-oiled, shiny wheels and the primed appearance of its levers.

Lucy invited him back to see the GRUB BUG. The girls walked on either side of him as he wheeled his chair towards the gate-lodge.

"Do you really want to be expelled from school?" asked Lucy. She was an obedient pupil with a healthy respect for school rules. Someone who broke them as flagrantly as Rich fascinated her.

"If they don't expel me soon I'll have to run away." He laughed, slapping his legs. They looked thinner than the rest of his well-muscled body. "And I'm not exactly in a position to do that."

Lucy blushed and looked away, unsure how to respond. It was the first time she had met someone in a wheelchair and she wondered how she should react. Should she feel sorry for him? But one look at Rich Harrison quickly dispelled that illusion. His manner was so natural that she found herself laughing back: "No, I don't suppose you could run away. But from the speed you came down Docker's Wharf I'd say you're a fast mover."

"He's the champ," agreed Sally in a disgusted voice. "No one's ever broken his speed record on the Wharf. But I'll do it yet. I bet you anything I will."

"That's strange," Rich said when Colin's Gates came into view. "I was never able to see anything in those gates before except weird squiggles. But now I'm looking at the shape of a girl. It's as clear as daylight. And what's that behind her? Is it supposed to be a wave or something like that?"

"It's mud," said Lucy. "She's running from a mud-slide."

"Is it...is it supposed to be Elsie Constance?" he asked. His voice sounded strained.

Lucy glanced quickly at him. "Do you know the story of Elsie?"

He nodded in reply, his expression guarded as he examined the gates.

After the disappearance of Mr Seagrave, the owner of the rock concert hall, Kate had organised the excavation of Colin's Gates from the river. The divers had expected a long search along the river-bed but, much to their surprise, Lucy had been able to pin-point the exact spot where they lay.

"How on earth did you know the location, kid?" Trumper, one of the divers, had asked her.

Lucy shrugged. "Oh! Just luck, I guess." She was growing used to keeping silent. Since the return of the gates to their rightful place, the image of Elsie Constance could be clearly seen by everyone. It was as if the disappearance of the ghostly child had removed the mystery from the gates. The wrought-iron bars no longer tingled beneath Lucy's fingers when she touched them. From the centre of the design a small heart was missing; instead it hung around her neck.

Rich was about to say something when Valerie came dashing out from the cook-house, almost knocking over his wheelchair in her efforts to hug him.

"Sit on my knee and give me a kiss," he ordered. She obliged with great enthusiasm.

"Don't let Alan Bradshaw see you doing that," smirked Sally.

"*Him!*" Valerie tossed her red hair. "What's *my* business got to do with Hogs Bradshaw?"

"Richard, you little pup. Are you back again to torment us?" asked Mrs Shine, puffing her way over to them.

"Sit on his knee, Mrs Shine, and give him a kiss," said Sally, trying not to giggle at the alarm on Rich's face as the large woman loomed over him.

"None of your nonsense, child. I'll shake his hand—and that's the proper way for a woman of my advanced years to behave." She invited him into the cookhouse where he sampled her apple doughnuts and Valerie's pizzas. He made moaning sounds of appreciation and gave a thumbs-up sign. Rich thought the garishly-coloured GRUB BUG was brilliant. He was introduced to Kate, a small, thin woman with hair bunched on top of her head who seemed to dance rather than walk around the cookhouse, checking everything and ignoring Mrs Shine, who was was ordering her to sit down and eat before starting the lunch-time run.

"So how's the anarchist?" boomed Old Knees-Up. "Still causing havoc at Leeside?"

Rich grinned at the old man, who looked as sprightly as ever, dressed in a track suit bottom and a GRUB BUG t-shirt with the words THE GRUB BUG IS AN ADDICTION BUT WHO WANTS TO BE CURED? written across it. He hugged Rich, his face crumpled with pleasure. Rich endured the probing and the muscle testing that Old Knees-Up put him through with a good-natured grin, flexing his arms so that his muscles rippled.

"Are you still doing your road-training every morning?" asked Old Knees-Up.

Rich's face clouded. "Let's just say they don't encourage it at Leeside. Everyone's too interested in rugby," he replied.

Old Knees-Up snorted loudly. "Rugby! Huh! Bums in the air like pigs at a feeding trough. Call that sport!"

"That's called a scrum, Mr Bradshaw." Rich was trying not to laugh.

"You can call it what you like, lad. But I call it a distortion of the human physique. God never designed the brain to be turned into a battering ram! You tell the powers-that-be at Leeside that rugby is *not* the kind of exercise that is the disinfectant of the mind and scouring wire for the soul." It was obvious that Rich, like all the others, had heard that particular saying many times. His lips twitched and when he saw Lucy looking at him their eyes lit with laughter.

"He's nice," she thought. "We'll have good fun with him over Christmas."

"Off with you now," ordered Mrs Shine, suddenly becoming very business-like when she looked at the cookhouse clock. "And you too, Sally Masterson. These young women have work to do. Lucy! Attack those onions."

Lucy groaned. Rich winked at her as he was leaving. "I'll see you later."

"Sure thing, Rich." She had made a new friend and for a short while as she chopped the hated mountain of onions she was able to forget about the red-feathered bird who haunted her dreams every night.

5
The Zentyre Meeting

"Order! Order!" demanded Alan. He was chairing the zentyre meeting that was being held in his laboratory. "Cut out the giggling, Sally. What's so funny all of a sudden?"

"It's Bodwin's Battler," she gasped. "It's like a walrus with cauliflower ears. And what's that thing hanging down underneath it? It looks like a...a...willy!" She collapsed against Valerie's shoulder, screaming with mirth. Everyone except Alan burst out laughing, although Lucy blushed furiously. Sometimes Sally was impossible.

Alan treated Sally's observation with the contempt it deserved. "That's a sound control lever. Professor Bodkin believed that the zentyre's chant could ultimately be defeated by ultrasonic sound. But the pitch must be so intense that it penetrates the mist and the power that lies beyond it. However, there is great difficulty in assessing the powerful forces of supernatural or psychic phenomena and converting them into a conventional scientific context, especially when the equipment involved is so archaic," he told them, in his best lecturing voice.

"What's that guy saying?" Sally begged the others.

"He's telling us that the old professor was as dotty as he is—and that he doesn't have a clue about what he's doing," explained the ever-helpful Valerie.

"Never mind, Alan," hooted Sally. "Where's there's a willy there's a way!"

This set them all off again. Alan was disgusted. It was difficult being a genius when the rest of the world had brains the size of peanuts. "In case it has escaped your attention we are here to discuss something very important—defeating the zentyre Solquest—which is what this machine is all about."

That stopped the laughter quickly enough. But secretly they all agreed with Valerie that Alan was just inventing for the sake of inventing. Bodwin's Battler had no credibility

The Zentyre Meeting

with any of them.

Zentyre Magic—Illusion or Reality? by Professor B K Bodwin, was an old book, a slim volume printed over fifty years ago. In its pages Professor Bodwin had tried to trace the elusive existence of zentyres. It was obviously a subject that had fascinated him. He had designed a machine for defeating the zentyre chant and drawn explicit diagrams and instructions in the centre pages. While the others avidly read his findings, Alan photocopied the drawings and set about finding suitable parts to re-create the machine.

So far he had managed to locate a weird assortment of items like rusting hollow funnels, cylinders, and an old gramophone player. The dock area had provided a rich source of broken-down, abandoned machinery.

Jumbles of wires, mirrors, tubes and valves littered his work-bench. Despite the scepticism of his friends he was convinced that he could build a machine that would be capable of drowning the low, hypnotic chant of the zentyre. But the others felt that the professor's findings were too vague to be of any help. He claimed to have located the island of Isealina and intended using his machine to defeat Solquest. If he was successful he would outline the details of his voyage in his next book. But no matter how much Alan searched, it appeared that no further book had ever been written by him.

As usual he insisted on outlining each detail of what he hoped to do. The others fidgeted and froze their faces into expressions of interest and eventually Valerie shut him up by shaking a can of fizzy orange and spraying the contents at him. When order was restored, and they had persuaded Alan to stop fuming, they each read from the notes they had made in those few precious hours after Solquest's visit to Merrick. It was like reading a book that had been written by someone else.

"Did we have to have a meeting tonight?" grumbled Sally, when her turn arrived. "Couldn't we have waited until after Christmas?"

"What's wrong with you now?" demanded Robert. But Lucy knew that they wanted to enjoy the festive atmosphere of their holidays instead of delving into things they were unable to understand. In Alan's house there were plum puddings hanging in muslin bags, presents under the tree and Christmas cards displayed on every available space in the lounge. There was something so unreal about sitting in a zany laboratory reading impressions from Robert's

The Zentyre Meeting

journal about zentyres and luvenders and a mysterious island called Isealina.

Paula claimed to be suffering from writer's block and had not produced any good work since the departure of Jon Freeman. Even if she had a poem ready she would not have read it because everyone kept looking at Bodwin's Battler and trying not to laugh. Sally's comments had completely ruined the solemnity of the occasion. Eventually an exasperated Alan called the meeting to an early halt. Lucy seemed far more relaxed than yesterday and was able to convince them that she was fine, perfectly fine. She lied with conviction, understanding the reason why her friends were so reluctant to read from the notes they had made about Solquest. Everyone was relieved when they joined hands and renewed the vow that Paula had written for them.

> *Let the courage of Elsie Constance guide us through the mist of Isealina.*
> *Let her wisdom help us overwhelm the enchantments of Solquest.*
> *Let her spirit protect us from his evil.*
> *Let her vision reveal the servants of evil to us so that we will always recognise the true nature of the luvenders.*

Just as they were coming to the last sentence Lucy glanced towards the laboratory window. She screamed, flinging her hands over her eyes. A distorted face with a flattened nose was pressed against the glass and staring in at them. Hands clawed the window. Puckered lips breathed circles of condensation on the glass.

"Rich Harrison! You big pig!" yelled Sally, who was the first to recognise him. They could hear him laughing outside as he withdrew his face and turned his chair towards the door.

"Quick! Hide the machine. I'm not having any funny comments from him," Alan hissed at Robert. The two boys threw an oil-stained blanket over Bodwin's Battler and shoved it underneath Alan's work bench.

"What were you lot up to, holding hands like that?" Rich asked when he came inside. "It looked like you were having a seance."

"Don't be daft. You're imagining things," said Robert, firmly.

"I am not! You were all chanting something. Come on, what were you doing?"

"Wishing each other a happy Christmas," said Sally, sitting on his knee and winding her arms around his neck. "Just like this." She kept smacking her lips against his cheek.

The Zentyre Meeting

"Hey get off, you sex maniac! This body is not for sale." Rich pulled back from her exaggerated kisses.

He followed them out of the laboratory, still chuckling. It was a dark damp night. The mist swirled around them like trailing cobwebs and the air felt stifling. Lucy drew a deep breath as the ground gave that crazy tilt beneath her feet.

"I've left something on the work-bench," she gasped. "Go on into the house. I'll follow you in a minute."

She hurried back into the empty laboratory and sat down on a stool, feeling a deep sense of aloneness as she leaned her arms on the bench, lowered her face into the crook of her elbow and closed her eyes. She could see the red-feathered bird, hear her plaintive cries echoing over the sea.

"Lucy, what do you know about this?" a voice asked. The image vanished. She jumped to her feet, stumbled and regained her balance. Rich Harrison had followed her into the laboratory. He was reading the piece of paper on which Paula had scribbled the zentyre vow. His good humour had disappeared. Lucy noticed how pale he had become, his lips barely moving as he whispered the words. Suddenly he looked older than sixteen years. He thrust the paper at her. "Tell me what this means!"

Lucy crumpled the paper and flung it to the ground. How could he be expected to understand? "What does it sound like, Rich?" she said. "Just a child's horror game. You know the kind of poetry Paula writes. It's nothing more than that."

"It sounds like much more than that. And you've got to tell me what it is!" he demanded. "This is no game for children." He tugged her hand, pulling her down on to the stool so that she stared directly into his eyes. "Please Lucy! Tell me what you know about the zentyre?"

There was something Lucy needed to understand about the boy who sat in front of her, something that Elsie wanted her to know. Yesterday Rich's face had tensed at the mention of the ghostly child, a fleeting secret glance that her mind had registered but had not thought about until now. He was scared.

She could sense his fear, almost touch it. And it was familiar, a reflection of her own fear when the image of Solquest crossed her thoughts and pulled at her heart. She instinctively knew that Rich was a person who did not frighten easily, yet his hands were clenched around the arms of his wheelchair, his knuckles

The Zentyre Meeting

were white and ridged with tension. He was asking her a question with his eyes and, when she returned his troubled gaze, she listened to the knowledge that hummed at the back of her mind and whispered, "You've been touched by the zentyre. Solquest came to you too."

Rich drew a deep breath, looked at her in amazement. "How could you know that?"

She shrugged. "Sometimes I just know these things. The knowledge seems to be wrapped up in my mind and just unwraps itself at certain times. It's...it's awful. I hate it." She spoke heatedly, as if some unseen force would hear her and take notice.

"As soon as I came into this place I felt that Solquest was hiding somewhere," Rich whispered. He looked ill, as if he would throw up over the floor. But he drew in a deep breath, releasing it slowly. The two of them glanced hurriedly around but there was nothing to frighten them in the zany laboratory with its wild murals and colourful ceiling.

Yet when she asked him to tell her what had happened, how he came to know about Solquest, he shook his head. "Not now, Lucy. It makes me sick as soon as I try to talk about it. I keep hoping I'll be able to get over this feeling but sometimes I think I never will.

Anyway it's not important. What's important is what's happening now! You've got to tell me why Paula wrote that crazy vow?"

With the mist drifting past the window and the wind making whispers in the trees she told him everything, not understanding why she should trust him, just instinctively knowing that she could. She told him about the mysterious happenings that had trapped them in the concert hall. She talked about Isealina and the strange ominous dome. The luvenders who scurried so swiftly over the ledged mulchantus garden. The bird that cried in the mist and filled her heart with foreboding.

When she fell silent he touched the piece of iron she wore around her neck, swung it to one side. There was a faint black mark in the hollow of her throat as if the iron heart-shape had branded itself on her skin. "The mark of Elsie Constance," sighed Rich. He released the pendant and sat very still for a moment, his head bowed.

"Did you ever wonder what it must feel like to fly?" He suddenly broke the silence that had fallen between them.

"Sometimes I do." Lucy sounded surprised at the change in their conversation. "When I see birds swooping over the river or watch them

The Zentyre Meeting

gliding in the air I try to imagine how the world must look from where they see it and... and...lots of things like that."

Rich was nodding as if he agreed with every word. "I never wondered about flying. But I used to wonder what it felt like to stand and walk and run and jump and how the grass would feel when it was crushed under my feet. There was a time when I couldn't think about anything else."

"Was that when you lost the power of your legs?" asked Lucy, who did not understand why Rich was in a wheelchair. She blushed, afraid that such a personal question would embarrass him. But he replied so matter-of-factly, without a trace of self-pity, that she quickly realised it was her own embarrassment she was projecting on to him.

"No. I've been like this since I was a baby. It was a car accident that damaged my spine. I'll never be able to walk." His eyes darkened. "It's tough. But that's the way of it. When I was younger I just accepted it as natural. Then at thirteen I got mad, really mad! People used to tell my mother that I was a cute little angel and they expected me to behave just like one. There was even one man who used to keep calling me 'God's little earthly angel'."

Rich snorted with disgust and Lucy giggled.

"So I started answering back and being terribly rude to anyone who patted my head or talked as if I wasn't able to understand them. Even if they thoroughly disliked me, it would at least make them recognise me as a real person. I was a bit of a pain in those days but I don't regret it one bit."

He shrugged the memory aside and she suspected that he was casually dismissing one of the most traumatic times of his life. She reached towards him and gripped his hand but he did not seem to be aware of her touch.

"Then something happened that changed my whole way of thinking." His voice dropped and he spoke slowly as if he was reliving a nightmare. When he looked up at her she could see the fear in his eyes but she also knew that he had come to a decision.

"Do you want to tell me about it now?" she asked. Her heart gave sharp skips of panic when he nodded. She did not want to hear this story. But the expression on Rich's face was one of longing, the need to share his experience was so obvious that she sat quietly, afraid to move in case it would disturb his concentration as he began to talk.

6
The Spectrum of Vice

"On the night it happened I'd had a row with my parents before going to bed," Rich began his story. "Actually, looking back to that time, I think I had rows with almost every person I knew. It took me a long time to fall asleep because I was so depressed and angry and confused over everything. I kept thinking about my life and where I was going with it and my thoughts kept spinning around and around in my mind without getting anywhere. When I finally fell asleep I had a really weird dream. It seemed as if all my anger was smothering me and I kept trying to shove it away and think clearly. But every time I pushed against the anger my hands touched something hairy and scratchy.

"When I woke up I thought I was dreaming

still because I felt a heaviness on my chest that I couldn't push away. A mist hung over the foot of my bed and I could see my hand in the silvery light that shone from it. My hand was moving as if it was in a slow-motion film and then it touched something on my chest... ahhhh!"

"You don't have to tell me any more, Rich," whispered Lucy, who wanted to run as fast as she could from the laboratory.

"No...no...I can't stop now." He pulled his hand free from Lucy's grasp and chewed his knuckles, his forehead furrowed with lines of fear. She waited in silence until he stopped trembling and lowered his hand. "The thing was alive. It was breathing and the bristles of fur on its coat were rough against my hand. There was a smell, a horrible, cloying smell that seemed to rise from the thing and when I touched it, it made a sound like...like... hicc-upping laughter. I couldn't breathe or move. I told myself that this was a nightmare, that I could force myself to wake up. Sometimes I can do that when a dream is really off the wall. But I *was* awake. I thought maybe a cat had come into my bedroom but when I looked into the red-centred eyes and the open mouth and saw these really sharp fangs I knew that there was no animal in life that could carry such evil on its breath.

"I screamed but it was a dream-scream, you know that little whimper you make when you're dreaming and you think you're really screaming your head off?"

Lucy nodded, unable to reply because her throat felt as if someone had been scraping it with sandpaper.

"I could only stare as the creature rose and stood on the floor watching me. But I could still feel the weight of the hideous thing on my chest. I could see the creature's claws and sharp talons and stubby fur and those awful... awful eyes watching me all the time as he scurried towards the mist and drew it apart like a set of curtains on a stage.

"When the mist parted, a tall man stood in front of me and bowed as if he was going to perform an act. He wore a white robe that fell to the floor and it had lots of gold squiggles on the front of it. The creature crouched at his feet and they both smiled at me.

"Then the man spoke. 'Follow me, Richard,' he said. 'Rise and walk behind the great Solquest.'

"I started to cry and kept telling him that I couldn't walk. He wouldn't listen to me.

"'Do as I say, Richard!' He repeated this command over and over again. His voice seemed to wrap itself around me and before I knew what was happening I swung my legs over the edge of the bed. The floor was cold beneath my feet. I felt strange and shivery and expected to topple over like a chopped tree. But my legs were steady as I followed Solquest and his creature from the room, down the hallway and out through the front door.

"The door swung outwards, away from us, pushing in the opposite direction from its hinges. There wasn't a breath of air stirring the blossoms on the cherry tree or disturbing the mist that followed Solquest. A dog whined and when that stopped there was utter silence. The bungalow where I live has a sloping lawn with high hedges all around the garden. In the centre of the lawn Solquest stopped and turned around to face me.

"'Does it feel good to have such power in your legs?' he asked, in this real soft, honey voice.

"'Yes,' I said and I was no longer trembling.

"'Run,' said Solquest. The grass was dewy and cool beneath the soles of my feet. My blood seemed to be on fire. When I reached the hedge I leapt up in the air, well above it, and then I was on the other side...running...running...

The Spectrum of Vice

running!"

This time it was Rich who held Lucy's hands. His grip was so tight that she gave a faint cry of pain.

"My body was like a machine, well-oiled, obeying my every command. Oh Lucy! It was so wonderful! When I returned to the garden Solquest stood in the same position. He stretched his hands towards me. I was glowing with excitement. But his hands were colder than sleet on the wind when he touched me.

"'Run forever, Richard,' he said. 'Take your destiny in both hands this night and shape its future.'

"'How can I do that?' I was beginning to feel afraid again. I pressed my heels into the grass and rocked back and forth.

"'Tonight I have come to offer you the spectrum of vice,' whispered Solquest. In his hand he held a flame. It flickered in seven different colours, like tentacles weaving together into such a bright spectrum that it should have dazzled my eyes. 'Look into the flame, Richard. Fill your mind with its power and it will burn strongly within you.' The flame grew brighter and brighter but I was still able to stare into it. The weird colours were separating, forming shapes of people, so many people, standing, holding up their fists in a victory salute, cheering, a roar of celebration that kept echoing inside my head. Then I recognised myself. I was a famous athlete. Everyone was rising to honour me as I ran a victory lap around a sports stadium. I knew it really represented the stadium of the world.

"I could see so many things waiting for me in the spectrum: years of success, gold medals, adoration, wealth, power. Then the picture faded. As if a soft wind blew a whirlpool of air through the spectrum the colours began to separate again, forming seven tentacles of orange and yellow and indigo and violet, wavering shapes of red and green and blue, each one beckoning me forward. I shrank away from them, knowing that if they caught me they would harm me in some horrible way.

"'Each colour represents my zentyre vices,' said Solquest, pointing to the coloured tentacles. 'Rage, cunning, cruelty, jealousy, vengeance, magical powers of evil and greed. Look into the spectrum, Richard and feel its power.'

"A buttery-yellow tentacle touched my hand. Suddenly I was consumed with greed, the desire to win, win, win...no matter what it cost! Then the blue colour flicked against my face

The Spectrum of Vice

and mindless waves of cruelty swept over me. The green tentacle was like a mist in my eyes and I was obsessed with jealousy. I would have destroyed everything in my life to satisfy this urge. Then I saw the red tentacle and lifted my fist in a blind fury, the fury of Solquest when he has been defeated. Orange colours burned my body with the heat of vengeance.

"Out of the corner of my eye I was aware of violet shadows darting towards me but disappearing so fast that I was hardly aware of them. That part of the Spectrum contained the cunning, hidden skills of the zentyre. Then a mysterious indigo cloud appeared, the final colour containing all the secrets of zentyre enchantment.

"'That is the last and most important of my zentyre vices,' said Solquest. 'My evil powers of bewitchment are safe within the mystery of indigo. But this is a power that I do not share with anyone.'

"He held the spectrum of vice close to my face. 'Everything else you can have, Richard. The years that you see unfolding within the spectrum belong to you, wonderful years when your name will be revered throughout the world as the greatest athlete of your time. Those who seek to run faster than you will be no more than a tremble in the wind. You will be invincible.'

"'And who will *I* tremble before?' I asked him, trying to turn my eyes away from the flame.

"'You will tremble only before me. As the servant of the zentyre, Solquest, you will never forget that I have given this, and more, to you.'

"'And what if I refuse your gifts?' I asked, petrified. I knew that if he commanded me to take the spectrum of vice from his hand I would not be able to refuse.

"The creature who was lurking behind him began to chuckle.

"'Silence, Irric, my luvender,' hissed Solquest. But he was also smiling, as if he could read my thoughts.

"'You are right, Richard. I can command you to take the spectrum. But I want you to take it willingly and, in doing so, to become my follower on earth.'

"His words terrified me. Yet, in a strange way that I could not understand, I was also growing angry.

"'You have shown me a vision of evil,' I shouted at him. 'I can only earn those rewards by using the vices that I see within the spectrum.'

"He kept staring at me and smiling his strange smile that was like syrup sliding all over his face.

"'Wise words come from your lips, Richard. But let us not waste time. Do you accept my gifts?'

"I don't know where my courage came from. But something happened to me as I stood facing him. I had crushed the grass beneath my feet when I ran, and felt that I belonged to the wind when my body soared into the air. Wonderful, wonderful feelings that I had always imagined. Suddenly, the resentment I felt because I had to live my life in a different way disappeared. I was being offered the dark gifts of the zentyre and I had only to reach out my hand. With that one gesture all my dreams could come true. Until that night I had allowed myself to belong to other people who kept doing things for me and making decisions for me and telling me that they knew what was best for me. This time, no one was guiding me or pushing me or thinking for me. But once I accepted the spectrum of vice I would belong entirely to Solquest. No power, no glory, would ever hide that fact.

"'I *will* be a great athlete some day. When that day arrives my strength will come from *within* me and not from the bewitchment that you offer me,' I shouted. Then my legs began to buckle and his laughter roared around me, or maybe that was the sound of the wind, rising.

"'Strength! What strength do you possess, foolish boy? You have one last chance. Do you willingly take the spectrum of vice from the great zentyre? Or will you return to the helpless anger that has consumed your life? Do so and you will not see the dawn overpower the darkness of this night.'

"Tentacles of flame continued to call me forward. If I reached out I would lose control over my own life, forever.

"'Choose, Richard!' Solquest shouted. He gripped my shoulders with bony fingers that dug into my flesh. I felt an ice-cold sensation as my skin seemed to wither beneath his touch.

"'*I choose not to walk*!' The flame fluttered wildly and was extinguished by the wind that began to blow wildly around us. I could no longer feel the grass beneath my feet. I placed my hands over my ears to drown the sound of his laughter. In those few seconds before I fell to the ground, I knew freedom, wonderful freedom that would run and leap and fly forever through my mind. 'I can do what I want to do,' I thought, as grass-blades scratched my eyelids and I lay still, trying to draw air into my lungs.

"The zentyre and his luvender had disappeared. Darkness was all around me except for the hall light that was like a beacon, trying to draw me back into the safety of my house. Sweeping sheets of rain turned the lawn into a quagmire. Each time I tried to dig my hands into the grass and pull myself forward it turned into mud that slid through my fingers.

"'Help!' I called. 'Somebody help me!' But the words stayed inside my head. Rain washed over me and flowed across the lawn until it looked like a lake of ice.

"'I won,' I kept whispering to myself as if the words could keep me warm. 'I chose not to walk. I chose freedom.'

"The wind tossed the cherry blossoms and they scattered around me like pink snow. Solquest was right. I did not see the dawn rise over the horizon but slipped into a coma and when my mother found me next morning my face was buried in mud. She told me later that it reminded her of a death mask.

"In the hospital they were unable to offer any hope that I would recover. For a week I lay unconscious with only vague memories of living in a world of shadows and hearing voices that seemed to float above my head. And always, always, that multi-coloured flame remained in front of my eyes, taunting me. The weight of the luvender crushed my chest. My shoulders felt as if they had been trapped in ice.

"At first there was nothing to mark the passing of time but after a while I began to recognise the shrill noise of day and the hushed, muted sounds of night. One voice came through to me more clearly than the others. It was a female voice, belonging to the night whispers, and it always reassured me. I also recognised the hand of its owner when she touched me.

"She came to me one night and removed the pyjama jacket from my shoulders. I heard her draw in her breath as if she was shocked but not surprised at what she saw. She traced her finger over the marks that Solquest had imprinted on my skin. 'I knew it,' she whispered. 'It is the mark of the zentyre. You poor boy. You poor brave boy.'

"There was something cool on my skin, an ointment that she rubbed into my wounds. I could smell flowers, yet I could not recognise the scent. It seemed to have the fragrance of

The Spectrum of Vice

every flower I had ever seen and the smell of grass when it is cut on a warm summer evening.

"The pain began to ease. After she left, the perfume still lingered in the air. When I inhaled the fumes, the brilliance of the spectrum began to dim in my mind. I drew in a deep breath and held it until I thought my lungs would explode. Only when the flame was finally extinguished did I release my breath.

"My eyes opened. The first thing I saw through the ward window was the wisp of a new moon in the sky. A beginning of life. Next morning a group of doctors came to my bed. They sounded very excited, talking about the wonders of modern-day drugs and telling me what a lucky boy I was.

"Dr Thorm, the night-duty doctor, came that night, an elderly woman with kind eyes. When she touched my forehead, I knew at once that she was my midnight visitor. Every night until I left the hospital she continued to treat me with the sweet-smelling ointment. After a while I was able to sit up in bed and talk to her.

"I told her everything about Solquest's visit and could feel my chest expanding as if the weight of the luvender had finally been removed from it. When I finished speaking she held a mirror before me and I saw where the grip of the zentyre had left shrivelled widths of skin on my shoulders.

" 'I have studied the lore of the zentyre for more years than I care to remember,' she told me. In her spare time she wrote books about supernatural things. Her third book was going to be called: *Thorm's Study of the Supernatural, Vol 3*. Zentyre enchantment was the subject for this book and she asked my permission to include my experience as a case-study in it.

"Of course I agreed and told her that I would never be able to repay her for her care and kindness. 'Do the other doctors know it was *your* ointment that cured me?' I asked. She began to laugh.

" 'Richard, do you really think for one moment that they would believe you had been touched by a zentyre? As it is they think I am quite obsessed in my search for proof of his existence. If they knew that I rubbed this ointment on your shoulders every night they would call me a mad witch and probably drive me out of the hospital. Not that that would bother me. I'll be retiring quite soon and then I'll spend all my time researching and writing.'

"My scars had faded but not disappeared by the time I left the hospital. She watched me getting into my wheelchair. 'How do you feel, Richard?' she asked me.

"'I feel strong!' I shouted. 'I feel ready to take on the world.' But I was unable to shake off the fear that some day Solquest would come after me again—and this time he would win. I got that feeling again tonight when I read Paula's zentyre vow. Whenever I get scared I visit Dr Thorm and she makes me feel strong again."

"She sounds like a wonderful person," whispered Lucy. His grasp on her hands had relaxed. Their faces almost touched as they stared at each other.

"I'm bringing her a Christmas present tomorrow afternoon, so why don't you come with me?" he suggested. "She lives at the very end of Merrick Docks and the supernatural still winds her up as much as ever. She'll blow your mind when you meet her. You must tell her everything that you told me. The others can come along as well."

"No, don't tell them anything," said Lucy, quickly. "I haven't mentioned any of this crazy stuff to them. I know it will frighten the life out of them and they think I'm weird enough as it is."

"Don't ever be afraid to be different, Lucy,"

said Rich. His voice had suddenly become husky. "Elsie Constance gave you something special. That sets you apart from the others whether you like it or not."

"What's going on here?" Robert interrupted their conversation. He was standing with Valerie at the door, looking very annoyed at the idea of Lucy and Rich Harrison holding hands and talking so intently together for the previous hour. But noting the warning glare from his sister he twisted his lips in a smile and said, "We're on our way home. We thought you might like us to walk with you to the GRUB BUG, Lucy."

"That's a good idea," she replied, rising to her feet. "Are you coming with us, Rich?"

"No. I want to talk to Alan about something. But I'll pick you up about noon tomorrow."

"Great. See you then."

"So where are you off to tomorrow with *him*?" Robert asked, trying not to sound too interested as they entered Merrick Mall where the GRUB BUG was parked.

"Nowhere important. Just somewhere around," explained Lucy, vaguely.

"You're a mine of useful information," he growled.

But she wasn't listening to him. She was

thinking of Rich Harrison, who had known the fury of the zentyre. Unlike her friends he experienced no relief from the memory of Solquest. Yet he had not allowed it to drag him down. On the outside he was full of fun and she would never have suspected there was anything wrong except for the stark terror she had seen in his eyes when he read Paula's zentyre vow.

They had poured out their fears to each other and had felt a sense of togetherness growing between them. It was not the flickering excitement she experienced whenever Robert moved close to her. Nor did it make them want to stake claims on each other and jealously guard them. This was something different and they did not need words to explain how it happened. Instinctively they knew that this feeling would never change, no matter how they changed, or how their lives changed and moved along on different rails. Even if they never met again, never spoke another word to each other, they would still be there, in a tiny pocket of each other's minds, two survivors who remembered.

7
The House on Jutting Toe Pier

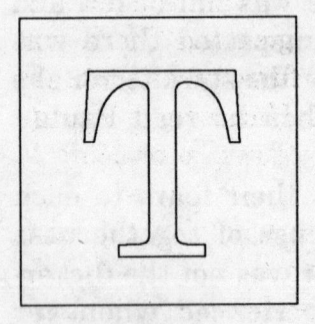

The following afternoon Mrs Harrison collected Lucy and drove to an area of the docks that Lucy had never seen. The wide walls edging the river and the buildings that lined the dock area eventually petered out about a mile from South Dock. Then a bank of land known as Jutting Toe Pier took over, dividing the water and ending at the point where the river and sea joined together.

Jutting Toe Pier was—as its name suggested—shaped like a rather scaly-looking toe with a bunion perched on the tip of it. On closer inspection the bunion turned out to be a house, narrow and curved like a miniature lighthouse. It looked down into the sea, its windows shining a welcoming light on dark nights when fishermen craved the comfort of human contact

The House on Jutting Toe Pier

on their long journey home.

Years of neglect had crumbled the brickwork on the pier, creating huge craters in its surface. Mrs Harrison complained bitterly about slashed car tyres and ruined suspension as they drove along. After greeting Dr Thorm, whose face crinkled into furrows of pleasure when she saw Rich, Mrs Harrison left to do some shopping in Merrick Town, promising to return in two hours.

Jutting Toe Pier was a lonely, bleak spot but Dr Thorm had resisted all efforts to persuade her to move. The back of her house faced the sea where an up-and-over boathouse door opened out onto a wooden jetty. This slanted into the water and was continually lapped, and often dashed, by waves. To the front of her house a garden formed an attractive horseshoe, with a crazy-paved pathway leading to the front door.

Dr Thorm ushered them into a small room where a log fire blazed. She was a small, hardy woman, with a face like a wrinkled map and grey cropped hair. Her constantly changing expressions reminded Lucy of a very lively monkey.

Some people called Dr Thorm an eccentric, others believed that she was a white healing witch. But she was neither, just a woman who understood the healing plants of nature and, since her retirement from Merrick General, people who were ill travelled great distances to seek her help.

While Rich made tea and toasted scones on the open fire Dr Thorm brought Lucy upstairs to a tiny attic room that she used as a study. Her desk, situated in front of the window, gave her a clear view of the sea but today that view was obscured by drifting mist. Lucy glanced down at a thick manuscript on the desk entitled *Thorm's Study of the Supernatural, Vol 3*. Dr Thorm had also written *Thorm's Study of the Supernatural, Vols 1 and 2*. These thick hard-backed books, occupied pride of place in Dr Thorm's bookcase.

When Lucy flicked over the typewritten pages of the manuscript Solquest's name seemed to leap out at her.

"Sit down here, my dear. You've turned very pale," said Dr Thorm, taking the manuscript from her and guiding Lucy to a chair. "I knew by the expression on Rich's face as soon as he arrived that you had something important to tell me. Now seems like a very good time to talk to me about it."

Lucy did not find it difficult to talk to Dr

The House on Jutting Toe Pier

Thorm. There was something strong and reliable about this elderly woman who sat so still and silent as Lucy told her story. She sensed the tremendous excitement of the doctor but her face remained calm and attentive throughout.

When Lucy finished her story Dr Thorm opened a desk drawer and took out a letter. "Read this, Lucy," she said, handing it to her. "My uncle wrote this letter to me fifty years ago. It will give you some understanding as to why I have been so obsessed with discovering whether or not the zentyre Solquest exists."

The paper was faded, creased and dog-eared from many readings. But the wide-spaced handwriting was still distinct.

The Round House,
Jutting Toe Pier,
Merrick Docks

Dear Niece

Today I embark on the most perilous journey that I have ever undertaken. It is ironic to think that I have travelled to the remotest corners of the world but have never before felt such apprehension. Yet my journey is short. I travel towards the Drowning Mist, that cloud of mystery which I continually see from my attic window.

In the past you have smiled, most politely and discreetly I will admit, at the vagaries of your eccentric old uncle who talks unceasingly about a source of evil called zentyre enchantment. I make no apologies for my obsession. I do believe in the existence of a zentyre—even though I have never seen him. Despite my many years of research I have acquired very little information on this mysterious zentyre. But I have a theory as to how he came to Isealina and that is why I built my house on Jutting Toe Pier. It offers me a distant view of The Drowning Mist.

When I lay down my pen I will guide my boat down the slope of the jetty. I will row towards this place and see if the island of Isealina exists beyond the mist's barrier.

For many years I have worked on the design of a sound machine with the capacity to emit an ultrasonic blast so high-pitched that it will shatter this commanding chant that I believe to be the voice of Solquest. It is installed

The House on Jutting Toe Pier

in my boat and I intend using its full force to penetrate this mist and defeat him. Even if luck does not favour my mission and the machine is destroyed, it will issue a warning that I am in danger. This will allow me time to row out of the mist before the zentyre chant lures me to my doom.

If I return in triumph I shall write the definitive book on zentyre enchantment for I realise that my first book, Zentyre Magic—Illusion or Reality? *is too vague to be of much use to the serious student of this subject. Sadly, if you are reading this letter, my prayer will have remained unanswered. Should this happen I have left instructions that all my possessions will belong to you. But I would rest more peacefully if you could find the time to read my research notes and, perhaps, in the future, you will write the book that I never managed to complete.*
Goodbye, my dear niece,
Your loving Uncle Bertram.

"The Drowning Mist," breathed Lucy. She shivered at the ominous sounding name. "But where *is* the Drowning Mist?"

Dr Thorm walked towards the window and stared out over the waves. "Sometimes on a clear day I can see it from here. It lies low on the horizon and seems to move in different directions. It is the fishermen who call it the Drowning Mist. They say it is caused by local currents or submerged rocks or hidden whirlpools or low-lying clouds. Even atmospheric conditions." She smiled, grimly. "Everyone has a different theory as to what causes it. The only thing that they agree on is that they should steer well away from it. Too many drownings have made them wary of investigating it."

"What happened to your uncle?" asked Lucy, staring out into the mist that lazily swirled around the little house.

"His doctor said he died from a heart attack, brought about by exposure and exhaustion," sighed Dr Thorm. "That was the official verdict given when they discovered his body. His boat had drifted, lost at sea for four days before it was spotted by the captain of a fishing trawler. My family believed that Uncle Bertram was an eccentric old man and never questioned this verdict. But I was unable to forget his letter and although I am interested in investigating all things supernatural, I have spent so much of my time trying to establish the existence of zentyre enchantment."

Dr Thorm lifted the manuscript of *Thorm's Study of the Supernatural, Vol 3* in her hand as if she was weighing it. "Do you know how much work went into writing this?"

Lucy shook her head.

"Three years and it is still not finished. But it has taken me fifty years of research, sneaking hours here and there to make notes, saving newspaper clippings of mysterious happenings around the world that might be linked to zentyre enchantment, doing interviews, reading my uncle's charts and diagrams and diaries, setting off on wild-goose chases across the sea, but always being afraid to venture too close to the Drowning Mist. Many, many times I wanted to dismiss my uncle's theories as nonsense and wondered if the zentyre really existed—or was his bleak, isolated life just a figment of my uncle's imagination?"

Dr Thorm was a woman who liked proof. She liked to touch things with her hands, to feel their substance, listen to their sound. Not exactly the type of woman one would expect to spend her spare time investigating the supernatural. She smiled wryly at Lucy. "But then I met the boy Richard." For an instant her wrinkled features softened at the memory of that first meeting. "He was in a trance but whenever I touched his face he whispered the name, 'Solquest'.

"The fear in his voice made me shiver. Richard was the first person I ever met who had been touched by Solquest and he bore the marks upon his shoulders."

"Where did you get the ointment that cured him?" asked Lucy, fascinated by the unfolding story.

"Come, I'll show you." Dr Thorm left the attic-room and led Lucy into a larger room where a curving window took up almost all of the wall. Potted shrubs, trays and barrels of herbs were growing everywhere, creating a tantalising pot-pourri of fragrances.

"What a lovely idea. An indoor garden!" exclaimed Lucy.

"It's more than that, my dear," replied Dr Thorm. "It's nature's pharmacy. All these plants and herbs have great healing powers and when people come to my house looking for cures these are what I use. Every summer I bring them outside to be touched by the sun and in the winter this is where they shelter from the winds."

The House on Jutting Toe Pier

Lucy gently touched the fragile, pale-green leaves of a plant growing from an earthenware container. "I've never seen that plant anywhere else but on the grave of Elsie Constance." She sounded surprised.

"You're an observant young lady," replied Dr Thorm. "And that's exactly where I found it. I took a tiny slip from her grave some years ago and much to my surprise it's been blossoming since then."

She told Lucy that she had discovered the white-blossomed plant on Elsie's grave by accident when she was researching her zentyre book. She was familiar with the story of Elsie Constance, who had saved the first band of workers on the dock-site from a mud-slide by shouting a warning. One cry was all she uttered before she died. People believed it was "Centre", a warning that the mud-slide would destroy their small cluster of cottages in the centre of the dock-site. But when Dr Thorm was introduced to Mrs Shine (of cookhouse fame) another version of the story was revealed to her.

"It wasn't 'Centre' that the poor child called out. It was 'Zentyre'," stated Mrs Shine. She claimed to be Merrick's top historian and had strange stories to tell about Elsie Constance, who in her short life seemed to have possessed the gift of second-sight, and the ability to read into the minds of people. But ever after her death her strange presence was reputed to have returned to Merrick Town at times of trouble.

"Not in a ghostly shape, you understand," explained Mrs Shine. "Elsie would never do anything ordinary or common like that. When she came back she used her ghostly voice and the person she chose to hear her words was always a young girl.

"It was said that she placed a little mark on her neck, like one of those beauty spots. An unusual kid was Elsie Constance—not everyone's cup of tea. But you must admit she had style."

Mrs Shine was a large woman with a commanding voice and looked quite belligerent when she was telling her story, as if she expected Dr Thorm to laugh and dismiss it as nonsense.

But Dr Thorm did not laugh and assured her that all things were possible. Together they climbed Merrick Heights and visited the grave of Elsie Constance. The wind was sharp and blew the long grass into twisted tufts, revealing delicate white blossoms that hugged the ground.

They triggered off a memory in Dr Thorm's mind and she removed a clump of flowers by their roots. When she returned home she planted them in an earthenware container and opened her uncle's book on zentyre magic. As she had suspected she saw his drawings of the white flowers called Healing Touch. The blossom and leaves were reputed to heal the withering touch of a zentyre's hands. The flower appeared rarely and did not seem to belong to any particular climate or terrain, but grew on a spot where a zentyre victim had been buried. They kept their pale scallop-edged leaves all year round but blossomed from May until September.

She did not think very much about them again until she saw the marks on Rich's shoulders. He was slipping out of life without a fight, only an occasional whisper of Solquest's name showing that he was still alive. The flowers, Healing Touch, shone like white stars in Dr Thorm's garden.

She crushed the leaves and petals to a pulp and massaged his skin gently with the ointment the following night. When the doctors marvelled at the speed of his recovery she smiled and said nothing to them.

On the boy's release from hospital he persuaded his parents to let him spend some time convalescing with Dr Thorm in her house on Jutting Toe Pier. It was time for her to retire from Merrick General and he stayed with her for a month, growing strong again under her care. He learned to relax, to allow his mind to live with the memory of what he had endured.

From her uncle's research Dr Thorm knew that victims who were fortunate to survive being touched by a zentyre normally could not remember the experience except in some cases when they had recurring nightmares. She believed that Richard's clear memory of what had happened came about through the regular application of the white-blossom ointment.

She had opened a jar of ointment and was showing it to Lucy when Rich shouted, "Scones are toasted. They're superb. Come and get them before I eat everything myself."

"Never tamper with the temper of a chef," laughed Dr Thorm. "Let's go join him."

The afternoon light was dulled, obscured by the mist that had thickened and seemed to press against the window. Log flames cast shadows on the walls.

"Will you tell Lucy what you have discovered

The House on Jutting Toe Pier

about Solquest's beginnings?" asked Rich when they had finished eating. Dr Thorm stared into the flames as if she had not heard his request. Her silence was easy. Lucy knew she would answer him in her own time.

"I think that Lucy has talked enough about the zentyre for one day. I will give her a copy of my manuscript. I know she will keep it safe and she can read what I have written about Solquest before we meet again."

Outside the round house Mrs Harrison gave a beep on the horn of her car. Two hours had passed since Lucy arrived. She wondered, not for the first time, why—when every ticking second took the same length of time to pass— time should move so slowly when she was bored yet fly so quickly when she was interested in something. She did not want to leave the flickering log fire and the comfort of Dr Thorm's presence. But she was helping Kate in the GRUB BUG tonight and Mrs Shine had mentioned something nasty about unchopped onions.

"I'll come to see you again as soon as Christmas is over," she promised Dr Thorm. "I'll look forward to reading your story."

The old woman with the wise monkey face hugged her and stood at her front door, waving to them as Mrs Harrison's car bumped and bounced along Jutting Toe Pier, slowly moving through the mist and heading towards the swinging Christmas lights of Merrick Town.

8
A Christmas Shopping Spree

Saturday morning dawned, dull and overcast. Three days to Christmas and Kate, as usual, had left her shopping until the last minute. As she did not serve lunches to the Little Dock construction workers on Saturdays she took the morning off and drove into Merrick Town with Lucy.

Lucy always looked forward to a shopping trip with her mother—and always forgot that such trips normally ended up in sulks and rows. It all boiled down to a matter of taste. Lucy was convinced that her mother had the most impossible dress-sense when it came to buying clothes for her only daughter. Kate thought Lucy's dress-sense was perfect, if she wanted to spend her life keening at a funeral. "Why does everything have to be black black and black on black?" she demanded on such occasions. "Why can't you wear something nice?"

"Because nice means collars and bows and pleats," explained Lucy, patiently. It drove Kate mad when Lucy trailed her index finger over endless rails of clothes, dismissing them scornfully without even attempting to try anything on. Or when Lucy dragged her mother into basements with black walls, loud rap music, ladder-stairs and crumpled heaps of clothes that, claimed Kate, had all been dyed the same shade of sludge-green.

After a few hours Lucy always began to sigh and sulk and slouch, furious with her mother, hating her reflection and the pimples on her forehead that always appeared just before a shopping trip. But peace was normally restored in The Coffee Grinder where they fortified themselves with cream doughnuts.

On this occasion they had two rows. One was over a mini-skirt that Kate maintained looked like a wide, studded, black belt in disguise. She thought that Lucy's choice of Christmas shoes was only suitable if her daughter intended taking up mountain climbing as a serious career option. Lucy said the shoes her mother wanted her to buy would look better on the

A Christmas Shopping Spree

top of a Christmas tree. Tempers were simmering when they met Jassy Masterson with her family of three in tow.

Simon, Jassy's youngest child, had been to visit Santa in Dunaways and was carrying his present, a large colouring book and paints. He had also received a tin of blowing bubbles liquid and was chasing rainbow bubbles along the paved, pedestrian zone. He looked happy and excited, unlike his two sisters, who had the same trapped expressions on their faces as Lucy.

"Teenagers," sighed Jassy Masterson.

"At what stage do you think they develop *taste*?" hissed Kate.

Lucy, Sally and Paula exchanged long-suffering glances and everyone went off to recover their tempers in The Coffee Grinder. Lucy paid little attention to the adult conversation until she heard Jassy mention her brother, Don Collins.

"I gather you had dinner together the other night," said Jassy to Kate in a voice that almost managed not to sound curious.

"We did," replied Kate. "It was a business dinner. We have a number of arrangements to make about the coffee shop."

"Of course," agreed Jassy. A polite silence

fell as each waited for the other to speak.

"I'm glad he's involving himself in this concert hall project," said Jassy when it was obvious that Kate was not volunteering any further information. "He led a very lonely life until he came back to Merrick."

"Oh!" said Kate in a voice that also almost succeeded in not sounding curious. "Why was that?"

"Too much work. Too much isolation in remote oil stations. Too much separation from his family. *Too* much time without a woman in his life. His wife died when Valerie was only two years old. And that's a long time ago."

"After Lucy's father died I certainly knew what it was like to be lonely," admitted Kate. "Even still I feel very alone at times." She looked quickly away when she saw her daughter staring at her.

Lucy was astonished. Kate lonely? Kate with the breezy busy manner who could never stay still for longer than two seconds at a time? Was she actually suggesting that she had something in common with Don Collins because they were both lonely? An incredible thought dawned. Did she fancy Don Collins? Robert's father! She could become Robert's sister! The thought made her want to giggle hysterically.

A Christmas Shopping Spree

"Catch on to yourself, Lucy," she scolded herself. "All she did was have a business dinner with him. That's nothing. Nothing at all."

Half an hour later she had changed her mind and wondered why, with so many *sane* mothers around, she had to end up with a total nutcase. It happened in Merrick Mall where Bella Donna, a spike-haired blonde in a leather miniskirt and black fishnet knee stockings, was busking with the Quados. The Quados had decided that a new image was necessary and Bella Donna, who called herself the Poisonous Poser, had joined the group as their female singer. They had started off singing Christmas carols but the sight of Bella Donna singing "Away in a Manger'" was too much for the average Merrick citizen who hurried past with averted eyes. So they had reverted to their usual style and the mall rocked to the beat of their music.

"Hey, look at the Quados' new act," said Sally, coming to a halt. The others obediently stopped and gathered around.

"Come on everyone—move those hips—get with the beat," yelled Bella Donna. She had black lines on her eyes and blue lipstick.

But no one was dancing on the tiled floor except Kate, who tapped her feet and swayed her shoulders and did a fancy bottom-wriggling movement as she listened.

"Act your age," ordered Lucy, who believed that her mother was the greatest show-off at times.

"Merry Christmas, everyone," said a voice. Don Collins was also doing some last-minute shopping with Robert and had stopped to listen to Bella Donna.

"That's a good solid rocking beat," he said. "It reminds me of my dancing days."

"Me too," said Kate. Her shoulders had started to sway again.

Lucy thought she would die, simply die of mortification, when Don Collins took her mother by the hand and led her out to the centre of the shining, marbled floor of Merrick Mall. The shame of it. And then they started to jive. Jive! Lucy had seen people doing that kind of dancing on television when they showed old-fashioned films. But television was one thing—Merrick Mall another. Yet here was her mother, her hair swinging loose from its topknot, not to mention her skirt almost swirling over her waist, doing all sorts of fancy hand movements. As for Mr Collins! He bent his knees and moved his hand as if he was conducting an orchestra and Kate spun around

A Christmas Shopping Spree

as if she was tuned into some secret signal in his fingertips.

The crowd cheered and whistled, while the Quados and their Poisonous Poser, Bella Donna, delighted to have some response, increased the noise and the tempo. Lucy could see Robert looking at the dancers, grinning from ear to ear. But the grin froze on his face as his father spun around and lifted Kate high in the air, swinging her to his left side—his right side—and then (with one accord all the young people covered their eyes) over his shoulder. Not once did he miss a step—and although the cheering population of Merrick Town really expected to see Kate sailing over their heads, she flew through the air like a butterfly and back into his arms again.

"It's unbearable," moaned Lucy, sinking her face into Paula's shoulder. "I can see her knickers."

Paula sympathetically patted her shoulder. "Yeah, but they're nice and fancy. There... there. It'll all be over in a minute."

"But will she be ashamed of herself?" demanded Lucy. She wondered when she would be old enough to run away from home.

"I somehow doubt it," replied Paula. "He's spinning her around now. Oops! How does he do that with his legs? Yippee! There she goes. Over his shoulder again."

"Ooooooh!" cried Lucy. "And she has the nerve to talk about *taste*!"

"It's really cool. I wonder if she'd give me jiving lessons," wondered Sally, bursting into loud applause when the dance ended.

"It's years since I did that," said Kate when she returned, sounding only a little bit breathless.

"I sincerely hope it will be years before you do it again," snapped Lucy.

But it was not all bad news. Kate had little energy left for arguing after that display. She wandered around the shops with Lucy, nodding vaguely when her daughter bought leggings and sloppy sweat-shirts and the black miniskirt that Kate had dismissed as short enough to be worn as a belt.

"I think you should dance with Don Collins every time we go shopping together," said Lucy when they returned, laden with bags, to the gate-lodge.

"Did I make a complete fool of myself?" asked Kate.

"Absolutely!" grinned her daughter, lacing up her fabulous ankle boots with the corrugated soles. "I think that's why I love you so

A Christmas Shopping Spree

much. Thank you for buying me such wonderful clothes."

Mrs Shine had taken a telephone call for Lucy from Jon Freeman. "He wants you to ring him back immediately you come home. Then you'd better give me a hand in the cookhouse. I need some..."

"Don't tell me," moaned Lucy. "Onions!"

"Got it in one, Miss Dosser," smiled Mrs Shine.

"Lucy?" drawled Jon Freeman when his mother called him to the phone. "Lucy who?"

She gritted her teeth. "Lucy Constance! You rang looking for me."

"Did I? Oh yes. Now I remember. I'm so busy it's difficult to remember every little phone call. Actually I'm ringing on behalf of my mother. She's insisted that I invite you over for a few days. You're to come on the 30th and stay over for this super bash I'm having on New Year's Eve. Everyone's coming. You can't afford to miss it."

"I'm sorry, Jon. I can't go. I've other plans."

"Those sorts of plans are made to be cancelled. This is the bash of the century."

"But I've got the finals of the Merrick Town Quiz on the 30th!"

"A quiz! You amaze me, Lucy. An actual

Freeman's Fancier with brain power? Joke! Joke! Ah, come on, have you no sense of humour? How about coming over on New Year's Eve then?"

"I'm going to a disco in the youth-club."

"Kid's stuff. What's the big deal about that? Don't tell me you're still going out with that creep, Bobaloo Collins?"

"The only *creep* I know is talking to me right now! Your Super Bash will have to manage without me because after the disco I'll be down on the river road celebrating Merrick 200 with my friends. Thank your mother—but tell her— no thanks!"

She smartly slammed down the phone.

"The H-less Wimp wants me to spend a few days in Lepping Vale," she told Valerie when she met her in the cookhouse.

"Ugh," shuddered Valerie. "I presume you told him to get lost!"

"Sure did!" said Lucy, briskly slicing an onion in two.

As always Christmas Day seemed to take forever to arrive—then flew by in a blur of presents and house visits and lazing in front of the fire with books and records and boxes of chocolates. Robert gave Lucy a fluffy white polar bear that growled; "You're so cute I could

A Christmas Shopping Spree

eat you up," when she turned it upside down. She bought him an ear-ring (he had recently had his ear pierced) and a calendar of Cold Command Charlie photographs. Earlier in the month she had posted it off to Jed, the lead singer. Each member of the group signed it and wrote a personal message on it to Robert.

Mrs Shine came for Christmas dinner. Lucy drank her first glass of white wine and wore her new mini-skirt. Old Knees-Up marched up Merrick Heights to celebrate Christmas and had to be rescued when he lost his way in the fog. On St Stephen's night Don Collins held a family party. He invited Kate and Lucy. They sang Christmas carols together, standing in a closely-grouped circle, and Lucy noticed how Mr Collins put his hands on Kate's shoulders and moved her to the front of the circle.

Then everyone sang a song on their own, played music or, in Paula's case, recited poetry. Lucy quivered in a corner and promised to die if she was called upon to perform. Robert played the guitar and sang "Sea Devil Eyes." Her stomach gave little skips of excitement when he looked over at her.

Thankfully there was no jiving and when she was finally persuaded to sing, she only went off-key four times.

Three days later the friends met in Alan's laboratory. This time there was no mention of the zentyre and Lucy did not tell them about her visit to Jutting Toe Pier. There would be plenty of time to discuss everything after Merrick 200. She had made a promise to herself that she would tell them everything then. They spent the afternoon cramming information for the finals of the Brains of Merrick Quiz which was being held the following night. Record vouchers were being handed out as prizes and they intended coming in first. But if their luck failed, second place would do. Rich volunteered to work the Christmas stodge from their brains by being quizmaster and questioned them for hours, mercilessly.

Lucy did the run in the GRUB BUG with Kate that night as Old Knees-Up was still suffering from the cold he had developed while wandering around Merrick Heights. It was midnight by the time she reached her bedroom. But she was not tired. She picked up Dr Thorm's manuscript and sat by the window in her wicker chair, staring out into the night. Normally the stars were reflected in the river, shimmering and dancing on the surface. But the mist took the lustre from them, hid them

A Christmas Shopping Spree

behind banks of heavy cloud.

She glanced down at the first page of the manuscript and hesitated. Since her visit to Dr Thorm she had deliberately avoided reading it, deciding to wait until after Christmas. "Well, Lucy Constance, there's no time like the present," she said to herself. For an instant her attention was distracted. Something low swooped over the water, then rose in staggered flight. The manuscript slipped from her hands and the pages scattered over the floor as her room seemed to explode with sound.

9

The Cry of the Red-feathered Bird

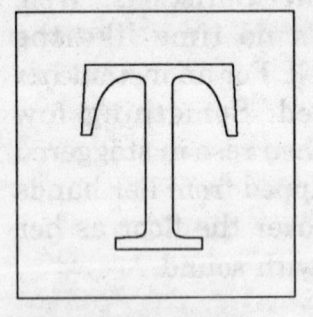

The cry broke the slumbering silence of the docks. A clamouring wail that came from outside Lucy's window. She looked out into the misty night. In the hazy glow of orange street-lamps she saw the red-feathered bird as she lurched, her belly skimming the river, wings drooping like a broken fan, making trailing patterns along the surface of the water.

"It's inside my head," she whispered. "It's another vision. I'll ignore it." Her hands shook as she tried to gather up the typed sheets of paper. The bird's cry rang out again. It echoed through the disused warehouses. Lucy threw *Thorm's Study of the Supernatural, Vol 3* from her, clamped her hands across her ears and closed her eyes tightly, as if this could crush the sight and sound of the wounded bird. But

The Cry of the Red-feathered Bird

when she looked again the bird was closer. Her wings barely moved. Somehow she managed to glide past the window, the red feathers touching the river. White eyes opened and stared straight up at Lucy.

"Help me," they seemed to plead. "Look at how I suffer."

The light in her mother's bedroom had been switched off, and the front door clicked softly behind Lucy as she left the gate-lodge. Colin's Gates opened silently.

Down by the river seagulls dived towards the red-feathered bird who was floating helplessly on the surface of the water. In a feeble gesture of defiance she beat at them with one wing, holding them at bay with her nightmarish shrieks.

Lucy clung to the jutting edges of the wall as she descended the moss-slippery steps to the river. There was a life-belt attached to a wooden holder. But when it was flung towards the bird it fell short. Again Lucy threw it out to the centre of the river. Again and again, until it looped over something, caught and held. As she pulled the rope and the bird drew nearer she gasped when she saw the object that had caught the life-belt.

It was a stake, long and thin like a fine

knitting needle, gleaming in a mother-of-pearl glow, and impaled in the chest of the bird. The life-belt held tight to the stake and soon Lucy was able to reach the bird and lift her from the river.

The small head lolled to one side. The bird's eyes were closed, covered by lashless eyelids. She was bigger than Lucy had first imagined, about the size of a full-grown swan. A dead bird, she decided. When she touched the strange weapon it burned her hand and she drew back, almost dropping the creature that hung so lifelessly in her arms.

The eyes opened wide. White eyes that bathed Lucy in their glare and seemed to plead with her. The crimson beak moved as the bird uttered a piteous whine that had lost the ferocity of its earlier shrillness. "Remove the weapon of Solquest. Please help me or I will die soon."

A bird that sang in human language! Lucy was beyond being surprised. Once again she touched the weapon, biting her bottom lip to prevent herself crying out as it burned her hand. It was impossible to hold her grip. She sank down upon the dock steps, and felt the damp moss penetrating the seat of her jeans as she examined the bird. A thin wasted body,

The Cry of the Red-feathered Bird

feathers dulled with dried blood. Once more she gripped the stake, closing her eyes to the agony on the bird's face, and her ears to the feeble pain-drenched whine, ignoring the burning sensation of scorched flesh on her hands as she breathed: "Help me to do this thing, Elsie."

Perhaps it was her imagination—because there was nothing to suggest any other presence except herself and the red-feathered bird along Merrick Docks—but a shadow passed over them as the pain eased, and she felt the same sense of calmness that always helped her to create pictures from the blackness. The stake came away easily, making a slurping sound as it withdrew from the bird's flesh. Her palms, which she had expected to be lacerated with burns, were unmarked.

Back in her bedroom Lucy washed the bird and searched the medicine cabinet for a soothing ointment to use on the wound. It was deep, an ugly gash that glistened when she touched the flesh surrounding it. Tears ran down her face as she imagined the journey of the bird, her desperate attempts to stay afloat as the pain consumed all her energy.

"Why do you cry, girl?" The harsh wail had been replaced by a musical timbre.

"For the pain you suffered," Lucy sobbed.

"It is only since the evil of Solquest pierced my body that I can understand such feelings," said the bird.

"Who are you?" Lucy rubbed her eyes. She fingered the delicate stake that she had removed.

"I am the Custodian of the Dark Rill, the river that runs through eternity. Once it trapped the zentyre, Solquest, but I foolishly allowed him one chance of escape."

Lucy shuddered and dropped the stake. It made a clanging sound as it rolled under her dressing table.

"You have good reason to fear the name of Solquest, girl," continued the bird. "I alone had the power to outwit him."

"Then why did you carry his stake of evil in your chest?" asked Lucy, angry with this mysterious bird who had brought the terror of the zentyre to life in her bedroom.

"Because I allowed my one obsession to overwhelm me. We gambled together and he won the battle between us." Her head drooped in shame. "I have been on a long journey, girl. A strange journey of discovery."

"What did you discover?" asked Lucy.

A sad smile touched the features of the bird.

"Pain. Such pain. And fear. I discovered a longing for life. I learned to hate the evil of Solquest and a desire grew deep within my heart to destroy him. I discovered shame that an obsession should control me—the Custodian of the Dark Rill."

Lucy's anger faded. She stroked the red feathers. The bird's eyes shone with emotion.

"These are strange feelings for a creature whose heart has moved like a stone through eternity. And when you touched me, girl, when you held me in your arms with gentle care, and your tears fell because I had suffered, I discovered the meaning of love. Then I learned to weep. Now I don't think I will ever be able to stop. Sleep, girl, for I have much weeping to do this night."

She began to cry, a silent grief that was only evident from the tears that flowed like a waterfall over her puckered timeless face. Lucy laid her on the cover of her duvet and climbed into bed beside her.

"I won't be able to sleep," she thought but, despite herself, her eyelids closed and she fell into a troubled slumber. On and off during the night she woke, switched on her bedroom light and saw the bird, still weeping.

"How many tears have you to cry?" she

asked as grey dawn-clouds sailed above the river.

"The tears of eternity," sobbed the bird. Lucy did not try to understand. When she woke again the bird was watching her from eyes that were glazed as cracked egg shells. But the tears had disappeared. Lucy inspected the wound. It was clean and healing; the gleam was returning to the red feathers.

There was a new energy about the Custodian of the Dark Rill that filled Lucy with foreboding. Sensing this, the bird sang soothingly to her. "Now it is time for us to talk, girl. So do not close your ears to my words. In the visions of your mind you have learned that Solquest will destroy Merrick Town. This town is like an itch beneath his skin. It will not cease until he is triumphant."

Lucy covered her face with her hands. It was happening again. Only this time there was no brief sensation of losing her balance or of being pulled into a centre of blackness that unfolded into mind-pictures. These pictures were clear, forming a completed jig-saw puzzle inside her mind. No—not inside her mind. The vision was taking place on South Dock, and all along the length of Merrick Docks. Images so clear she could have been looking at them in a glossy colour magazine.

New Year's Eve. Everyone in fancy dress. She could see Valerie in her clown costume, hundreds of brightly coloured dots on shimmery material. Robert was banging an enormous drum, dressed in a ragged coat covered in bright-coloured buttons. Clumps of fruit hung around his wide-brimmed hat. He was dressed as Sam Sparry, an old man from Merrick history who had beaten his drum when the *Triumph* sailed up South Dock on that first voyage two hundred years before. She had helped him create the costume and this afternoon would help Valerie sew the sparkling spangles onto her clown costume. Alan was there also, barring his fanged teeth in a vampire snarl, swinging his black cloak dramatically towards the Masterson sisters who were dressed in sailor suits, replicas of the costumes worn by the first sailors to sail into Merrick. With Valerie they were dancing a clumsy hornpipe on the river wall. Rich was a king, splendidly crowned, his wheelchair transformed into a throne. Lucy recognised herself in the crowd. Robert had handed one of the drum-sticks to her and she was beating a frenzied rhythm on the drum. She wore a long black wig and a swirling patched shirt, dressed in the image of the ghostly child, Elsie Constance.

From her bedroom window Lucy could almost touch the excitement on the river road at South Dock. It reminded her of the arrival of Cold Command Charlie last September. But when she thought about the events that followed that night she shivered because she could smell it, that same foul dead smell of mulchantus wafting over the crowd and no one, not even Lucy Constance, seemed aware of it.

Then it happened. Without any warning, the mist swirled over the river, swallowed the crowds, the warehouses, the half-completed buildings, the *Triumph* with its billowing sails, in a silver glow. Even the sound of bells, pealing joyfully from Merrick Cathedral, the frantic rhythm of Robert's drum and the last murmurs of children were absorbed and silenced. Lucy saw the heart of Merrick, its people, imprisoned in this silver cloud and the only sound was the throbbing beat.

"Heart of Merrick, keep beating!" Lucy pleaded as the sound diminished. Slowly, so slowly it ceased, a gentle rapping pulse that faded into a sigh of surrender. The mist lifted. She could see the eyes of Solquest, the glow of triumph surrounding him like an aura. The

The Cry of the Red-feathered Bird

river continued its gentle flow. The docks lay deserted in the early morning sunshine and over Merrick Town an unbroken hush greeted the first day of the new year.

"He is going to destroy us!" Lucy cried. "On the night of Merrick 200 the mist of Isealina will crush the heart of Merrick."

"This mist has already been hanging over Merrick for many days, but the touch of a zentyre is subtle and people are not yet alarmed," sang the bird.

Lucy stared out the window at the trailing vaporous wisps, an army of spectres floating over the town. She remembered the stifling feeling of breathlessness that she had experienced outside Alan's laboratory.

"He has broken his promise to Elsie Constance and she is no longer here to protect us. What can we do...what can we do?"

"You must destroy him, girl! You have great courage and it has been strengthened by the vision of the ghostly child. Now you also have me by your side—a bird of passion and vengeance. A bird who has learned to hurt. We will travel through the Dark Rill on our journey to Isealina." There was such a sweet melodic lilt to the bird's voice that it was possible to imagine she was singing a lullaby instead of uttering words of terror.

"I don't want to go to Isealina." The thought made Lucy's legs tremble because she knew that the bird spoke the truth. She had carried this knowledge in a corner of her mind since the first vision came to her. "Even if we do manage to get there, how can we destroy Solquest?"

"You have seen the island in visions," sang the bird. "You are familiar with its terrain. But there is only one way to enter Isealina safely. If I take you through the mist it will weaken my power. But I am strong in my Dark Rill and you will be safe with me. We will make our way to the tribab where the crystals of Ulum lie. These precious crystals have a mysterious earth energy that creates the enchanted mist when they are released into the atmosphere. We must steal the crystals of Ulum on the night of New Year, when Solquest renews his vows of eternal youth. As he steps into the water we will imprison his youthful form forever. His luvenders have only one existence—to serve the zentyre. They will also perish in the mist."

Lucy moved towards her bedroom door, knowing that once she left her room she would run forever, far away from the fantastic melody of the bird, and the visions that filled her with a sense of doom.

"You cannot escape your fate, girl," sang the bird. But where once there had been indifference in her eyes, they shone instead with kindness when she recognised Lucy's fear. "Our plan must remain a secret between us. You will go to Isealina accompanied only by me. Do not tell your friends of your departure. They are brave, but they are also foolhardy, and will try to follow you. I cannot bring them through the Dark Rill or they will be imprisoned in its grave of eternity. They have only one way of entering Isealina, by venturing through the mist. If they do so Solquest will destroy them instantly..."

"But I may never see them again. Or Kate! Or the GRUB BUG...or...or...!"

"Do not tremble, girl. Be still and allow your courage to possess you."

"I have no courage," cried Lucy. "It belongs to Elsie Constance."

"You are wrong, girl. It was not her courage that drew the stake of evil from my chest. It was your courage. Yours alone!"

Alone! Alone! Alone! The word rang with loneliness, stripping away the comfort of her bedroom with its white wicker chair and colourful duvet with "Cold Command Charlie" printed on its cover.

The Custodian of the Dark Rill suddenly arched her chest and spread her wings. She began slowly to fan them back and forth, creating a cool breeze that wafted across Lucy's flushed face.

"Tonight we will travel through the Dark Rill. It is a timeless place but by your human hours it will take us two spans of light and darkness to reach Isealina. Once we have the crystals of Ulum, Solquest will be under our control. You will be free from him forever. Now, tell me this, girl. Where is the highest summit you have ever climbed?"

"Tower Rock," said Lucy without hesitation, remembering the famous Lepping Vale landmark. The rock jutted from the sea at High Tide Bay and had been her favourite diving spot when she lived in the seaside village.

"Then that is where you will meet me tonight," commanded the bird. "To enter the Dark Rill it is necessary to ascend from the highest point that you have travelled in your young life."

"But how can I explain to Kate and the others? They'll wonder what's happened to me. And what about the team for the quiz and the disco...and everything?"

"You will give your reasons. You will tell the truth—that you are going to Lepping Vale for a visit. Sadly you will have to embellish this truth so that they will believe you. I leave that to you. Good, you have ceased to tremble, girl. Now tell me if you trust me? We will depend much on that trust in the journey before us."

"Yes," said Lucy, realising that she meant it. She grew calm and felt her fear subsiding, swept away in the fanning rhythm of the bird's wings.

"Now I will return to the Dark Rill and rest. I will renew my strength for the battle that lies ahead," promised the bird. She tapped her beak against the window pane and when the window was opened wide, glided gracefully away. Lucy rubbed her eyes. There was nothing in the sky except low-lying grey clouds and a red streak that glowed for a moment in the hovering morning mist.

10
Embellishing the Truth

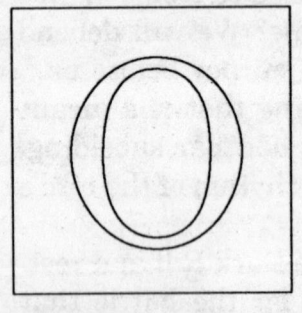

Only Robert was at home when Lucy rang the doorbell. Initially she had thought of ringing him, giving him a terse message and hanging up before he could start asking questions. But somehow the urge to see him had won out. She had rehearsed her excuses carefully as she cycled over the cobbled stones on the river road. The cars drove slowly through the centre of Merrick. Hourly fog warnings were issued on local radio.

Lucy followed him into the kitchen and told him that she was going to Lepping Vale for a short visit. She stared at the kitchen tiles and explained everything in a reasoned, logical way. She had not seen any of her old friends since moving to Merrick and believed it would be a nice gesture to celebrate the New Year with

Embellishing the Truth

them. A stubborn look settled over Robert's face.

"But you can't go to Lepping Vale! Not this week!" His tone was so authoritative that Lucy bristled with indignation. But now was not the time to argue, she decided.

Once again she realised how strange it was to lead a double life, one filled with mystery and fear, and another one full of everyday ordinary things like broken promises and disappointed friends and the uncomfortable feeling that she was telling a lie—or, as the Custodian would say, embellishing the truth—and not embellishing it very successfully to somebody who was refusing to accept it.

"I don't understand you, Lucy. One minute you're blowing hot, then you're blowing cold. Yesterday you were all talk about the quiz and all the info we'd crammed together. Now, without any warning you're letting down the team—and not even apologising for it. And what about the disco tomorrow? We were supposed to go together. And Merrick 200? We've planned so many things!"

"I'm sorry. I really am! But we've just got to unplan them."

"Just like that?"

"I said I'm sorry, Robert. I'm visiting Lepping

Vale—and that's that. I'll be back before you've even had time to miss me."

"Valerie told me the H-less Wimp rang you up. Are you staying with him?"

"Actually no. It's his mother who invited me."

"Huh! That's a handy excuse. I knew this had something to do with H-less and his Super Bash!"

"Don't be so childish!"

"Hasn't it?"

"I don't have to answer those questions, Robert Collins. You don't own me. I can go wherever I like without having to ask your permission."

"I know that. But I thought we were...well... something!"

"Why! Just because we kissed a few times?"

"Yeah! Does that not mean anything!"

"No! It doesn't. And it certainly doesn't give you the right to hang a sign around my neck saying 'Private Property'."

"That's fine with me." His disappointment was giving way to annoyance—rapidly. "And when you come back from Lepping Vale, if you do desire to honour us with your company again, don't look out for me 'cause I'll not be hanging around. I've had it up to here with

Embellishing the Truth

you. First I catch you kissing *that* wimp. And what about Rich? The two of you have been looking *very* cosy lately and every time I ask you anything about it you just choke me off. What am I supposed to think?"

"Think what you like, you pompous prat! I've had it up to here with your jealous moods. Get lost!"

"I suppose I shouldn't expect anything better from a Freeman's Fancier," he yelled, looking sick as soon as he had uttered the words. Lucy's face crumpled. When he put his arms out towards her she pushed him away and flung open the kitchen door, almost tripping over Valerie whose arrival home had remained unnoticed by the two of them.

Kate was surprised but much more reasonable when she heard the news that Lucy was leaving. "I thought you were looking forward to going to the disco with Robert? And all those other things. Have the two of you had a row?"

"I hate him."

"I'm sure you do. But the million dollar question is—will you still hate him tomorrow?"

"Yes! Oh yes!" said Lucy, with absolute conviction.

"Mmmm! Maybe you will and maybe you won't. But this sudden decision to go to Lepping

Vale must have knocked him back a bit. And what about your friends? Aren't you all on the same quiz team tonight? We were going to drop along and give you moral support."

"Who's 'we'?" asked Lucy.

"Don...I mean Mr Collins."

Lucy glared suspiciously at her mother. "Him! Don't tell me you're having another business meeting. Or maybe it's a dancing class this time?"

"Don't be so smart, young lady." Kate smiled that infuriatingly secret smile. "It's my night off and there are a lot of business details about the coffee shop still to be ironed out. If you're going to Lepping Vale you'd better check the train timetable. There's no way I'm going to be able to run you over. I'll ring Pearl Freeman and arrange for her to pick you up at the other end."

"No...no! I'll organise that," said Lucy, hastily.

Mrs Shine rushed into the gate-lodge in a frenzy, claiming that Kate had forgotten to order cooking oil and castor sugar before Christmas, an accusation that Kate emphatically denied. Within a few minutes the GRUB BUG team were reduced to their usual organised hysteria.

Embellishing the Truth

In the silence that followed Kate's departure, Lucy moved upstairs to her bedroom and inspected her face in her dressing-table mirror. Surely there should be some signs of change stamped upon it. She no longer felt like Lucy Constance who blushed easily, was eager to be liked, quick to feel insulted and in need of a large dollop of self-confidence. Instinctively she knew that she was still all of those things but somehow, since the visit of the mysterious red-feathered bird, that comfortable, familiar part of her personality had been tucked away on one side of her mind. In its place a new determination had grown, fuelled by the mysterious sense of vision that had been left to her by Elsie Constance. She would destroy Solquest. It was as if her links with the zentyre went back, far far back in time, and she could feel his evil all around her. But despite such thoughts and plans, her face still looked the same, her green eyes calm. Only her mouth revealed the extent of her fear, stretching into a grimace when her foot touched the stake that she had pulled from the bird's chest. It lay beneath her dressing table and she kicked against it, rolling it underneath and out of sight.

Kate dropped her off at Merrick Station and

saw her safely onto the Lepping Vale train. She ran along the platform as the train began to move, waving and calling out last-minute instructions to Lucy.

"Give my love to everyone in Lepping Vale," she shouted. "And hurry back to me. I'll miss you."

"Not as much as I'll miss you, Kate," whispered Lucy and began to cry. "Enjoy yourself tonight," she sobbed. "I like Mr Collins. I really do."

"You've a funny way of showing it, darling," called Kate. "But thanks anyway."

It was only after the train left Merrick and winter sunshine lit the carriage that Lucy realised how much her eyes had become accustomed to the foggy atmosphere hanging over the town. It was dark by the time she reached Lepping Vale. She walked swiftly through the small seaside village, head down in case she was recognised. But there were very few people about, and those who were paid no attention to the slim young girl, whose head was shaded by the hood of her parka jacket.

She thought she would feel sad when she saw the outlines of Cliffway House, where she had lived from the time she was born until last summer when she moved to Merrick Town. But

Embellishing the Truth

it looked different. The new owners had painted the outside of the house a gaudy pink. Posh new pillars had been placed at the front entrance.

"Yuck!" said Lucy in disgust, remembering its comfortable, ramshackle appearance and the once wild meadow that was now a tidy lawn with orderly rows of shrubs and paving slabs.

Even blindfolded she would have been able to make her way through the meadow and on to the cliff walk. But the moon hung low above the distant trees, lighting her way as the cliff path wound downwards, sometimes veering off into meandering side-passages. She stayed with the main trail that led to High Tide Bay. This was a small cove, ideal for swimming because of the depth of the water. Even when the tide was out it still held enough water to dive with safety from the highest rock.

"You did well, girl," said a familiar voice. Moonlight touched the bird's feathers, burnishing them with a bronze sheen as she dived towards Lucy. "You do trust me, girl?" She asked the same question again, moving her head quizzingly to one side.

"Yes," whispered Lucy and coughed, her voice hoarse with fear.

"Then climb swiftly to the summit of Tower

Rock," ordered the bird. "We have no time to waste."

The sea whooshed over the sand as Lucy began to climb. It was a familiar scramble, her feet sliding confidently into seaweedy footholds, the surface gritty with tiny shells of long-dead sea creatures. She was breathless by the time she reached the summit and stood poised, looking out over the sea and, turning around, seeing the twinkling lights of Lepping Vale. The bird perched beside her on the rock and, as she had done the previous night, arched her chest. Her wings began to fan the night air. The current blew Lucy to the edge of the rock.

"Close your eyes, girl," commanded the bird. "Remember, you are now flying on the wings of trust."

11
Spacer's Strange Behaviour

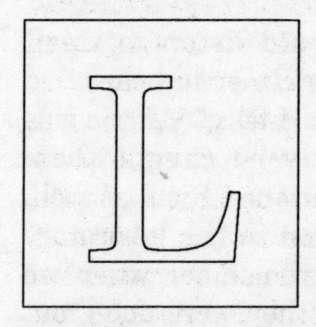

Lucy's friends could not believe that she had decided to visit Lepping Vale. The Masterson sisters and Valerie helped each other with their fancy dress costumes and tried to figure out why she had let them down so abruptly.

"She had a dreadful row with Robert this morning," confided Valerie. "They were in the kitchen and didn't hear me when I came in the front door."

"You mean you listened?" said Paula in a shocked voice. "You actually eavesdropped on them?"

"Yes."

"How could you do that?"

"By putting my ear to the keyhole," explained Valerie.

"I meant how could you do such a sneaky thing?" Paula tended to be very moral about such issues.

"Go on, Valerie," urged Sally. "Tell us. What were they fighting about?"

"I don't think we should listen to this!" scolded her sister, moving closer to hear.

"He was going on about H-less," Valerie was unrepentant. "Apparently he caught them kissing once. And he mentioned Rich, as well. How they were carrying on in the laboratory the other night. Do you remember when we were all wondering what they were doing out there?"

"That was very strange," admitted Paula. "They seemed really close when they came out. Only it wasn't *that* kind of closeness." She paused, following her train of thought. "It was as if they shared something special. But it wasn't *that* kind of something special. Like the feeling they had towards each other would never change—only it wasn't *that* kind of feeling. Do you know what I mean?" As a poet Paula believed herself to be a judge of sensitive human emotions.

Her friends nodded, completely bewildered.

"These trousers are awful," moaned Paula, trying on her sailor suit. "They make me look like a marshmallow."

"More like a cream doughnut," decided her sister, helpfully.

"Thanks a heap." Paula glared and Valerie waved her hand at them to be quiet as the front door slammed. "Would you look at him—the walking wounded," she hissed when her brother came into the room, accompanied by Rich and Alan. They had been playing snooker at Mad Harry's, the local snooker hall and it was obvious to the girls from the expression on Robert's face that the game had been a disaster.

"What are you lot talking about?" he growled, staring suspiciously at them.

"Nothing much," replied Valerie, carefully inspecting her costume.

It should have been an enjoyable afternoon. They played records, swotted up on quiz questions, and Valerie served them spicy chicken wings that ran tears from their eyes and left their mouths feeling like the inside of an active volcano. But somehow time dragged. They all felt edgy, uneasy, as if something unspoken troubled them. Maybe it was nerves over the quiz that would be taking place in a few hours. Or perhaps it was Robert, silent and moody, who made them more aware that Lucy

Constance's sudden departure was casting a shadow over the afternoon. "For goodness sake! It's not worth getting into such a state over her." Alan was growing impatient with Robert's mood. "This is supposed to be fun week, remember."

"I'm having a ball," growled Robert. "I don't know what you're talking about."

Later in the evening they met in the town hall for the quiz. Even though Rich, who had been dragged in to replace Lucy at the eleventh hour, performed heroically, their team of six lost by twenty points. This uninspiring display of combined brainpower placed them neatly in the middle, well beyond any hope of record-voucher prizes—or self respect. Every time they found themselves unable to answer a question Robert muttered, "*She* would have known that!"

By the end of the quiz Lucy was the hapless scapegoat with sole responsibility for their defeat.

They travelled home by bus. Buses always angered Rich, who was forced to depend on his friends to help him on board. He cursed loudly as he banged his elbow and glared at a woman who turned around to frown at him.

"Oh stop getting into such a knot about it,"

said Paula, settling into the seat beside him. Helped by Valerie, she had hauled his wheelchair on board. "You know we don't mind giving you a hand."

"That's not the point," he complained. "If you lot weren't here I wouldn't be able to use this bus. Why can't they build buses with ramps that can be lowered from the platform—and a proper place for people to wheel their chairs?"

Ramp Rule OK was Rich's motto, a world in which he and his wheelchair had complete mobility. He had become quite expert at organising demonstrations on such issues and Paula was one of his most committed rent-a-crowd supporters when the occasions demanded her presence and her placard. She had even written him a protest poem called "No Ramp Blues". But as the bus left Merrick Town she seemed distracted, making "yes" noises to everything Rich said.

"You're not listening to a word I'm saying!" He nudged her, feeling aggrieved.

"That's true," she replied, without thinking. "I...I...mean...yes I am!"

"Liar!"

"Sorry, Rich. I've got things on my mind."

The others also sat silently, only muttering "goodnight" to Robert and Valerie, who were the first to end their journey. Rich was staying over in Alan's house for the night. The downstairs room that Carol Bradshaw used as a study had been turned into a bedroom for him. Instead of staying up for a while and playing records the two boys said goodnight to Mr and Mrs Bradshaw, then headed for their separate rooms. On a few occasions during the night Rich woke and realised that his heart was beating rapidly, an uncomfortable sensation that made him sweat and push the bedclothes from him. Once he heard sounds coming from Alan's room and sensed the same restlessness in his friend.

Towards morning he fell into a heavy sleep. He dreamt that he was travelling on a speeding bus, houses blurring, people staring in horror as the bus bore down on them. Screaming at the driver to stop, slow down, you'll kill them! The smiling face of the bus driver turning around and Rich was looking into the blue mysterious eyes of Solquest. Rich rang the bell—rang and rang and rang—until the shrillness seemed to explode inside his head and he awoke, jerking from sleep to stare groggily at the telephone that was loudly ringing on Carol Bradshaw's desk.

"Is that Alan?" The voice sounded terse, very

Spacer's Strange Behaviour

terse. It was also vaguely familiar.

"No. This is Rich Harrison."

"Oh...hello, Rich. Kate Constance here. If Alan's around I'd like to have a word with him—fast!"

At Kate's end of the line Rich could hear a dog howling, a long-drawn-out doleful sound that set his teeth on edge. This too had a vaguely familiar ring to it. Alan, pyjamas rumpled, eyes sleep-rimmed, came into the office, yawned and picked up the phone.

"Hello, Kate. What's up?" He sounded sleepily curious but quickly snapped to life when he received a shrill verbal battering on his eardrum. Rich listened to the one-sided conversation.

"He's what! Oh yes, I can hear him all right! Was he really going on like that all night?" Alan winced at Kate's reply and held the receiver away from his ear, muttering to Rich, "I'll murder Spacer. This time I really mean it. The stupid mutt!" He returned his attention to Kate. "I'm sorry, Kate...OK! OK! I'm on my way to collect him."

"Whew! She's one hell of an angry woman!" he said, replacing the receiver carefully as if it might explode in his hand. The two boys made their way into the kitchen. It was 8 a.m. on

New Year's Eve, dull sky, clammy atmosphere, and a heavy mist that the weather forecaster hoped would lift by noon.

"That stupid dog got out and spent the night howling in front of the gate-lodge. Can you believe that? He can't open the side-gate so he must have jumped the wall. Why would he do that, especially when it's so high?"

"Was he here when we came home from the quiz last night?"

"Now that you mention it, I don't think he was," said Alan. "He didn't come charging up to us the way he always does. But I just thought he was asleep. Apparently Mr Collins brought him back here from the gate-lodge around midnight. But as soon as he drove off Spacer made his way back to the docks again and spent the night serenading Kate. No wonder she was mad. I bet she wouldn't have yelled so much if Mr Collins had been doing the serenading."

The two lads chortled. Since they heard about the dancing episode the relationship between Don Collins and Kate Constance was a subject of much speculation.

"It's strictly *business*," Robert had glowered at them when Sally brought up the subject in his house yesterday.

"Oh yeah! Just like you and Lucy," Sally smirked.

"Wrong!" Robert had snapped back. "Ours is strictly nothing!"

Alan opened the fridge and inspected its potential breakfast contents. Satisfied, he removed slices of bacon, sausages, tomatoes, eggs, white and black pudding and left-over boiled potatoes, a grapefruit from the fruit rack, a packet of breakfast cereal from the press and a loaf of bread from the bread bin.

"Are you sure that's enough, Alan?" asked Mrs Bradshaw, dashing into the kitchen on her way out to work. "I'd hate to see you suffer from malnutrition."

"It's nice of you to be concerned, Ma," he said, adding another sausage to the mound of food. His mother groaned, threw last-minute instructions at him and disappeared.

As Alan had a tendency to grill everything so that it became overdone and inedible, Rich manoeuvred his wheelchair over to the cooker and prepared breakfast. Alan rubbed the sleep from his eyes and slumped over the table. "What on earth made Spacer go over there? If Lucy hadn't vanished by herself it would make some sort of sense. But she's not even at the gate-lodge. Unless..." His voice hesitated as he stared down at his plate, then he made a face as if the sight of his food disgusted him. He left the room abruptly.

"Aren't you going to finish your breakfast?" demanded Rich in the voice of an outraged chef, when Alan returned with his duffel coat on.

"No, no. I'd better get down to the docks and collect the stupid mutt."

Rich scraped the contents of Alan's plate into Spacer's scrap-bowl and tidied the kitchen. Something was wrong. He was convinced that Lucy Constance's abrupt departure troubled his friends. Yet, when he thought logically about it there was nothing to worry them, apart from Robert's reaction which, when it was all boiled down, was nothing more than jealousy. Lucy had gone to Lepping Vale to visit this H-less horror and that was her business. He did not need to panic and shiver inwardly when he looked out the kitchen patio door at the mist. For an instant he saw something shining through it, many colours weaving a pattern and forming a spectrum that seemed to draw him forward. It faded as suddenly as it had appeared and he shuddered, cursing his overactive imagination. He was relieved when Alan returned with a sheepish-looking Spacer dragging his tail between his legs.

"You should see the fog down on the river. It's really something else. I can't see the *Triumph* sailing at midnight unless it clears up," said Alan. Once again Rich stared out at the mist. The trees in the garden looked distorted, stretching bare branches into the grey day.

A review of the year's sporting highlights was on television and the boys settled in for an afternoon's viewing.

Later, when Robert called around, Rich was surprised at his appearance. Yesterday he had looked fed-up. But today he was exhausted, his eyes red-rimmed as if he had not closed them for twenty-four hours. When he heard about the dog's escapade his expression grew even more disturbed. "That's not like Spacer. Remember the last time he howled like that? I couldn't sleep last night thinking about it. I read over the notes we made...and the dreams..!"

"Leave it out, Robert. There's no reason to think like that," snapped Alan.

"I know. It's just...! I shouldn't have gone on at her like that. I've been ringing H-less but the line is engaged all the time."

"He's having his Super Bash tonight," Alan's drawl was high-pitched and affected. "It's probably engaged because all his guests are ringing to cancel."

Robert grinned, but after a few minutes he went out to the phone in the hall. They could hear him dialling, then putting the receiver back with an impatient slam.

"Temper! Temper!" said Sally, who had called in to see if she could take Spacer for a walk. "I'm so bored. Paula's gone into one of her poetic moods and she won't talk to anyone. I need a bit of exercise to clear my head."

Rich was in the kitchen at 7.30 p.m. when Sally returned, upset and breathless. "I just took the lead off to give him a run in the park and he disappeared in a flash. I've searched for ages and I can't find him anywhere." She swung the lead distractedly, tears brimming, dreading Alan's reaction. "Where can he be?"

"I've a pretty shrewd guess that you're going to find out very soon," admitted Rich.

As if on cue, the telephone rang.

He did not recognise the voice at the other end of the line. But he recognised the tone— and the howl of a dog in torment. "Listen to me, young man! This is Mrs Shine from the GRUB BUG Company and I have a very unwelcome visitor on my hands. At this moment in time your dog is lying outside the cook house and his verbal antics would put a tribe of

Spacer's Strange Behaviour

banshees to shame. I want you over here this instant to remove him. Do you understand me, young man?"

"Yes, Mrs Shine," said Rich, meekly, and replaced the receiver.

"Alan!" he yelled.

"What is it?" Alan appeared on the landing with a tube of Trustyle Gel in his hand. His hair looked as if it had been electrified.

"Spacer's escaped again."

"You're joking! *Not* the gate-lodge?"

"The very place."

"I'll KILL KILL KILL HIM!"

"I think it might be better if you collected him first."

"How can I? We've got to be down in Valerie's in twenty minutes. It's going to take at least an hour to get down to the docks and back again." Robert had already returned home to prepare for the disco and Sally had slipped quickly away as soon as she saw Alan.

"Look, I'll go down to the gate-lodge and collect him," offered Rich. "I'll meet up with you later."

"Thanks a million, Rich. You're a real pal." Alan disappeared back into the bathroom.

Rich travelled swiftly in his wheelchair. Soon he had left the centre of Merrick Town behind and could see the misty outlines of the docks in the distance.

"I'll have to get back into a regular workout," he thought, feeling his arms beginning to ache on an upward climb. He planned to do the Merrick marathon in August and knew that his training schedule had been slipping since he had started in Leeside College. He heard Spacer before he saw him. The desolation in the dog's cry added to his uneasiness.

"Get him out of here before I string him up." Mrs Shine was at the end of her tether. She pointed an accusing finger at Spacer, who lay on the ground with his face buried in his paws. There was such misery in the expressive brown eyes that Rich's heart melted. But Mrs Shine remained unmoved. "If Kate comes back and hears that racket again she'll have him impounded and it would bloody well serve him right. I'm driven demented, I am, with all his carry-on. Go on, get the lead on him and get him out of here."

"Em...Mrs Shine...I em...came out in such a hurry that I forgot the lead!"

"Is it a brain you have in your head or a sieve? Go on over to the gate-lodge and see if there's a piece of twine that you can use."

The gate-lodge echoed with the hollow ring

Spacer's Strange Behaviour

of an empty house. Spacer accompanied him, panting rapidly, his nose quivering as he sniffed the kitchen floor. Rich found some twine in one of the presses and put it in his pocket. He was about to leave when Spacer began to howl again.

"Oh shut up!" he shouted, feeling his blood freeze at the eerie cry.

Spacer was standing at the foot of the spiral staircase that rose from the centre of the lounge. Rich looked upwards but he could see nothing. "What is it with you, anyway?" he asked the dog. In reply Spacer bounded up the stairs, his hind quarters wriggling as he rounded the narrow staircase.

"Come down immediately!" roared Rich in his most authoritative tone.

In reply Spacer poked his head between the staircase bars, as if taunting the boy below in the wheelchair.

For five minutes Rich coaxed the dog. But to no avail.

"You're going to pay for this!" He gritted his teeth and eased his body from the wheelchair. Step by step he hoisted himself up the stairs, using his arms as strong levers, conscious of the black dog watching him. On the landing he reached out to grab him and Spacer nimbly moved out of reach, treading dainty ballerina steps in the direction of one of the bedrooms.

"Your days are numbered!" warned Rich as he manoeuvred himself across the landing. "At the very least it's the mincing machine for you."

He paused at the bedroom door, his eyes immediately registering Lucy's personality: Cold Command Charlie posters on the walls, rows of books, tiny pig ornaments, an enormous polar bear on her pillow, face creams and tins of talcum powder. There was a charter of human rights for all young people under fifteen pinned to her door. Dr Thorm's manuscript was scattered on the floor beside the window.

Spacer crouched beside the dressing table, whimpering.

"What is it? What is it?" Rich felt his temper exploding as he pulled himself over to the dog. A voice growled behind him. "You're so cute I could eat you up."

"Oh shit!" He collapsed with laughter as the polar bear fell from the bed and landed upside down on the floor beside him. Then he saw a long thin object under the dressing table. His hand automatically closed over it as if it was a javelin. He balanced it, feeling the familiar thrill run through him as his muscles clenched and he made a mock-throwing gesture. But he

Spacer's Strange Behaviour

knew it was not a javelin that he held so expertly in his hand. He stared at the object, remembering pictures he had seen of underground caves of stalactites, realising that the object must once have descended from the ceiling of a cave. There was something on its surface, a smear, as if it had been hurriedly cleaned but not carefully enough to remove the last vestiges of blood.

His hand touched something else, his heart beginning to thud when he saw a long slender red feather lying on the wooden floor. The red-feathered bird. Lucy had talked about haunting wounded cries in the mist. He lifted the feather, beginning to tremble as it curled slightly with the heat from his palm.

Spacer whimpered. "Oh you stupid mutt!" Rich dropped both objects as if they stung him and pulled the dog close, burying his face in the soft black coat. "Come on, you carry it, Spacer," he whispered to the dog, trying to place the stalactite in his mouth. The dog's lips curled back, and for an instant he clenched his teeth against the strange-feeling object.

"Come on fellow, give me a break! I need my hands for climbing down the stairs," pleaded Rich.

Spacer obliged.

There were those who said that Rich Harrison's technique of descending stairs would put the heart of a kamikaze pilot crossways. He placed both hands on the bannister rails and swung himself from step to step, performing the whole exercise in a breathtakingly short time.

At the bottom of the stairs Spacer dropped the stalactite as if he could no longer bear the feel of it between his jaws. Back in his wheelchair Rich propped it up beside him and opened the front door.

"What kept you?" Mrs Shine was still feeling aggrieved. "I asked you to find a bit of twine, not weave a ball of it."

"Has anyone heard from Lucy since she went away?" he asked. Mrs Shine inspected a batch of freshly-baked bread rolls.

"Not a word. Kate tried to ring before going out on the evening run but the line was engaged all the time." She picked up an apple doughnut, lightly dusted it with sugar and handed it to Rich. "Be on your way, young man, and make sure that dog doesn't get out again or there'll be skin and hair flying."

Spacer whimpered and walked close to the wheels of Rich's chair. He panted rapidly, his tongue pulsing with the effort of breathing.

Spacer's Strange Behaviour

Rich felt his chest tighten as the mist filled his nostrils and his world was a muffled silver cloud that followed him through Colin's Gates and all along the cobbled river road of Merrick Docks.

12

Lucy Arrives in Isealina

Lucy stood on the summit of Tower Rock and felt herself soaring into the night. It reminded her of half-dreams, of the drowsy seconds before sleep arrived when her body seemed to shoot upwards from her bed and fly like an arrow through the roof of the house. Normally when this happened she would give a startled jerk and open her eyes to familiar surroundings, clutching her duvet cosily around her shoulders, then lazily drifting off to sleep.

This was no dream sensation. The force of her ascent was so ferocious that she thought her body would crash through the crown of her head. Upwards, ever upwards, until all sensations left her: no weight, no bulk, just pure effortless speed. The black void gave way to gold-streaked flashes of light. Perhaps they were stars, but she kept her eyes tightly closed and her faith in the red-feathered bird never wavered. When it seemed impossible to go any faster, for surely then she would shatter into many pieces, she began to slow down. Immediately she was caught in a more gentle rhythm, swaying backwards and forwards as if she was being nursed in the arms of the wind; and the bird sang sweetly all the time.

When she opened her eyes she was standing on the banks of a narrow stream, enveloped in dull grey light.

"Welcome to my Dark Rill," sang the bird.

Dead trees hung misshapen branches over the rill but cast no reflection on the water. Through the gloom that seemed to linger forever on the edge of dawn, Lucy could see the blurred shape of the bird as she flew past. She followed, walking along the timeless bank of the Dark Rill. Her feet touched the ground, but it was still like a dream-walk, a hazy journey to nowhere. Time ceased to have any meaning. When she looked at her wrist-watch the hands were missing. The numbers had faded. The rill stretched onwards like a dull ribbon, straight and unbending. She did not feel tired. The music of the bird seemed to carry her along so that, without her first realising it, her feet began to move faster. Gradually the trees with their hunched branches started to thicken. She could hardly make her way between roots that coiled above the ground like wart-flecked snakes.

The rill was coming to life, tiny ripples giving way to swirling eddies, keening sounds rising above the song of the bird. The Custodian's voice could no longer be heard above this growing clamour and she fell silent. Soon a high-pitched wailing filled the narrow rill. It terrified Lucy. She began to tremble, to stumble as if the strength had left her legs. She had imagined that the cry of the red-feathered bird was the most frightening sound she ever heard. But it was a lost whimper compared to this howl of fury.

"What is it?" she cried out in desperation. In her preoccupation with the keening noise Lucy had not noticed the rill shaping into a Y, the water splitting and veering into two separate streams with an embankment dividing them and running through the water like a black girder. It reminded Lucy of Jutting Toe Pier and she wondered if the Dark Rill flowed in some kind of mystical parallel to the river of Merrick Town.

Lucy Arrives in Isealina

The bird's wings had widened, outstretched in a supple glide, embracing the new directions of the rill. "Come join me, girl, and you will have your answer," she sang.

Although it looked like a great distance Lucy leapt easily over to the newly-exposed thread of land. The ground was stony and cratered beneath her feet. In one stream she could see flickering lights moving slowly in front of her. The keening reached a crescendo as she drew closer to them; the colours strengthened, burst forth and blazed upon the dreary half-light. For an instant Lucy thought that the kingdom of this strange bird was on fire.

As her eyes grew accustomed to the colours that flickered and throbbed and keened, she realised that on the surface of the rill there floated many flames, each flame blazing in a spectrum of coloured light. "What are they?" she cried out.

At the sound of her voice, the keening abruptly stopped. The silence, coming from either side of Lucy, seemed to crash against her eardrums.

"They are the spectrums of vice," the bird replied. "They are haunted spirits who cannot rest easy in death because in their human lives they accepted the spectrum of vice from the zentyre, Solquest."

Lucy remembered the terror on Rich's face when he spoke about the spectrum. She also remembered her own confrontation with Solquest, standing face to face with him on the deck of the *Salty Sara* while the strains of the Cold Command Charlie concert floated across the river towards them. She knew the power of the zentyre's voice, how it had mesmerised her mind and turned her thoughts towards evil ways.

"Perhaps they were unable to refuse the command of Solquest," she said.

"Solquest did not mesmerise them with his mind-power," sang the bird. There was no pity in her song. "They could have refused him but made a willing choice to accept the spectrum that he handed them. It became an invisible part of their personalities, a flame that never died throughout their long lives and brought them riches and fame beyond their wildest imaginings.

"They had everything they desired except love. For in accepting the zentyre's spectrum their lives were forever marked by the evil within it. When they died they still could not escape. The spectrum that had imprisoned

Lucy Arrives in Isealina

their spirits in life refused to free them in death. Each person was consumed by their flame of many vices and they are forced to flow forever through the Dark Rill, releasing their fury in an endless dirge because Solquest bewitched them. They have forgotten that he gave them free will to refuse his spectrum. They took from him willingly."

"Must they stay here forever?" Lucy asked, shivering as she tried to imagine a timeless existence, broken only by a keening frenzy and the weight of dead trees.

The Custodian, as if affected by Lucy's melancholy, sighed deeply. "They must never escape from the Dark Rill. If they are released, their freedom will only last for a brief instant in time. But they will destroy all that stands in their path. I, who was created to guard them, will then no longer be custodian of their fate. I will cease to exist. No, girl. The melody of life beats strongly within my chest. Until that beat ceases they are doomed to the Dark Rill for ever."

Upon these words the wild lamenting broke out afresh. Pent-up fury vibrated in the spectrums. Lucy trembled at their energy, sensing the desire deep within them to join together and consume her in one enormous multi-coloured flame.

It was growing increasingly difficult to walk and the dream-like feeling of struggling towards something that always remained out of reach was increasing. The wailing dirge faded away as the grey gloom returned.

Suddenly Lucy reached the end of the embankment. "Hold tight to your trust, girl," sang the bird. "We are now entering the island of Isealina."

A gasp of wind hurled Lucy forward. She was falling into darkness, choking on the overpowering smell of rotting seaweed, hearing the thud of waves crashing against rocks. With relief she saw the gleam of red feathers beside her as she staggered to her feet. But the bird no longer sang. Her feathers trembled in a rippling spasm.

"Are you frightened?" whispered Lucy.

The bird nodded her head. "If fear makes the heart race like a bird when it hears death roaring from a gun then I will admit to experiencing an emotion that must be akin to it."

Lucy's legs trembled so much that she did not believe they could hold her upright. The bird, seeing her distress, whispered, "But what of the courage that flows from a clear spring

Lucy Arrives in Isealina

within you? Use your fear to make you cautious and your courage to achieve success."

Gaunt rocks surrounded Isealina but the enchanted mist cast a glow over the island. Further inland, a river ran like a moat around the base of an enormous, craggy hill.

"Jump over the river, girl." The command came urgently from the bird who glided above her. "Solquest's power is waning as the time approaches for his ritual ceremony of eternal youth. But we are still in great danger from him."

As in the Dark Rill, Lucy seemed to float effortlessly over the river. Three green stones gleamed in a bed of clear water. They were now at the foot of the hill where flowering ledges rose upwards like circles of steps surrounding a high moss-covered dome. It seemed to stare like a giant eye, watching the young girl and her mysterious singing companion.

"That is the home of Solquest and his luvenders," sang the bird. "It is called a tribab and the crystals of Ulum lie within it."

The glow from the mist guided Lucy's footsteps but it could also expose her to unseen forces. Above her the mulchantus plant gleamed and she shuddered in revulsion as the scent wafted around her.

"We must swiftly reach the shelter of the mulchantus gardens," advised the bird. "The scent of the plant will disguise our presence and the leaves will save us from detection."

Lucy climbed upwards, moving surefootedly along the rocky steps. When she was three ledges below the tribab she ducked under the bronze rough-furred leaves, quivering as they brushed against her face. Thorns scratched her hands. But she forced herself to stay still.

An entrance had opened in the tribab. She could see grotesquely-shaped creatures with thin legs and a scurrying walk. These were the luvenders, erupting from the tribab with gulping sounds of pleasure, spilling out over the ledges, scurrying down towards her hiding-place, grasping leaves in their claws and sinking their sharp side-teeth into the pulpy texture. Solquest stood at the entrance to the dome, staring down over the island. The golden glow from the symbols on his robe shone like a ray of sunlight over the mulchantus garden. The Custodian of the Dark Rill lay motionless between the bronze leaves, her feathers dulled in a perfect camouflage.

Lucy felt no such security as warty claws clutched a leaf beside her face. She stared at

Lucy Arrives in Isealina

the razored nails and stubby fur. Surely she could be seen by the unblinking eyes that gleamed through the leaves? But the luvender scurried away and disappeared back through the tribab entrance. Solquest had also retreated from view. Sweat trickled into Lucy's eyes and she raised a hand to wipe it away. Clammy tendrils of pink-streaked hair clung to her forehead.

The tribab entrance remained open, casting forth the golden glow from Solquest's robe. Because of this light Lucy did not at first realise that the mist no longer shrouded the island. The sea was visible, waves whipping the rocks and sending sheets of spray into the air.

"Solquest has covered the crystals of Ulum," the bird told her. "The mist has also disappeared from Merrick Town and now the people will emerge to witness the festival of Merrick 200."

Lucy thought about her friends dancing to the music of Bella Donna and the Quados. She wanted to howl like a lost child but the warning expression of the Custodian's face made her clench her fists and try to remain calm.

"Soon the night will split into a new day. Soon the old year will die in the arms of a new year." Sweetly, softly sang the bird. "When Solquest comes to the river to bathe we must enter the tribab and remove the crystals of Ulum."

"I can't go into the tribab. I can't go into the tribab." Lucy whispered the words to herself.

"Breathe deeply and listen to the voice of your courage," whispered the bird. "It speaks wise words. We cannot retreat now."

Once again the tribab was alive with activity. The yellow glow intensified as Solquest emerged from the entrance, his white robe falling to his feet. The luvenders led the procession towards the river. Solquest slowly followed them.

"It is time to move, girl," the Custodian of the Dark Rill sang softly in Lucy's ear. "Solquest is ready to bathe."

Lucy moved from her hiding place and swiftly clambered up the last three ledges towards the passageway. Spiralling steps, carved into the craggy limestone walls, led her down into the centre of the tribab. Above her Lucy saw the high-domed ceiling with rows of hanging stalactites. Some were sculptured into barrel-shapes, tapering inwards as they descended. Others looked like fine icicles on a

Lucy Arrives in Isealina

window ledge. They glowed with a waxy ice-lustre. Moonshine, entering the tribab from an unseen opening, was reflected within them so that the ceiling appeared to glow with light from a thousand chandeliers.

In the centre of the tribab she saw the slab of rock on which the glass orb rested, a filigree of swirling mist patterning the sides. Lucy descended the last step, her foot jarring painfully as it touched the uneven floor.

"Remove the crystals of Ulum," hissed the bird, her voice trembling as she glided above. Her wings cast a dark shadow over the floor of the tribab.

Lucy's fingers clutched the glass orb, clumsily gathering it against her chest. She could hear the throbbing rhythm of the crystals beating in time to her own heart, restlessly tapping against the walls of their glass prison.

"Quick. We have no time to lose." The tempo of the bird's melody lent wings to her feet as the young girl ran across the tribab floor and began to climb the steps. Her breath rasped in her throat. She was filled with a wild sense of exhilaration. "I will destroy his evil. I have the means to destroy him."

Like the petals of a flower the glass would

open in her hand and the escaping mist would trap the zentyre and his luvenders forever. The moon emerged from behind a cloud. It hung in the black sky, full and rich as a shiny coin. On the river bank the zentyre raised his hands in the air and cried.

> *Stones of endless day and night*
> *I will bathe in your light*
> *As you enfold me in the youth of eternity.*
>
> *Let age bow swiftly from the race.*
> *And take the seasons from my face*
> *As you enfold me in the youth of eternity.*
>
> *When midnight strikes on moonlight's chime*
> *Release me from the coil of time*
> *As you enfold me in the youth of eternity.*
>
> *Leave no past to scar my thoughts.*
> *My date of birth is endless noughts*
> *As you enfold me in the youth of eternity.*

Lucy Arrives in Isealina

*Give me the strength of evil chains
To bind my schemes with zentyre reins.
And you—my three green precious stones—will enfold me in the cradle of eternity.*

Waves continued to crash upon rocks and answer to the call of tides. Minutes still beat a steady rhythm in time. But the silence over the island of Isealina was absolute as the chant died away. Lucy poised at the entrance of the tribab and looked down towards the river where the zentyre was preparing to bathe. His robe lay on the river-bank and the symbols glowed upon him as he stepped into the water. The bird hissed, swooped before her, tried to turn her eyes away. "Don't look, girl. I implore you. Don't look down."

But it was too late. Before the zentyre's eyes rested on her, the Custodian of the Dark Rill flew into the tribab and Lucy found herself, frozen with horror, unable to move, as she stared at the true form of Solquest. The fine-featured man who had stood so arrogantly by the side of the river had disappeared. In that instant, as he stepped into the water, Lucy saw the evil manifestation of the zentyre: his face a mask of oozing flesh, eaten by millions of translucent insects that moved over his skin like a swaying, devouring army. No features on his face remained, only gaping caverns of pitted bone and something that had once been his mouth stretched tightly in a smile.

Then the vision disappeared as the water steamed and rose in a vapour over his body to remove the face of evil. The zentyre's youth had been restored. Lucy's moment was lost. The glass orb rested uselessly in her hands as Solquest returned to the river bank. He stroked his beard, smooth and black like a raven's wing. When he stared upwards towards the tribab, his face was as if carved from the finest marble. "Welcome to Isealina, Lucy Constance. I had planned a surprise for your wonderful town. But instead *you* surprised *me*."

The luvenders had risen at the sound of their master's voice. In less than the flash of an eyelid they surrounded Lucy, scratching eagerly at her clothes, glaring at her from red-centred eyes. Their teeth glistened like the sharpest stalactites as they licked their lips.

Lucy screamed and screamed again. The suppressed fear she had felt when the first vision came, when she tried to remove the stake from the bird's chest, when she had

Lucy Arrives in Isealina

listened to the bird's lilting voice outlining the plan to enter Isealina—all her reactions to these mysterious happenings were included in the screams that echoed around the island. Solquest laughed. As the sound died away she became aware of a great feeling of calm and something else that made the blood rush to her head and clenched her hands into angry fists. It was her courage returning.

"Touch the face of a nightmare and it will disappear," she whispered. Holding tightly to the glass orb with one hand she reached out and swung her fist towards the luvender nearest her. The creature gulped in surprise and staggered backwards, tumbling down into the mulchantus garden. Then her hand was gripped tightly. She struggled, kicking out at the zentyre but all the time Solquest continued to laugh and mock her with his cold blue eyes as her struggles became weaker and finally ceased.

"Oh no, my pretty one! As a guest in my home you must know that this is not the way to show respect to your host."

"I came to Isealina to prevent you destroying Merrick Town," replied Lucy, amazed that she still had the strength to answer him.

"And how did you intend to do that, my

pretty one?"

She stared at her feet and did not reply.

"Since you do not answer my question I will have to find my own answers," said Solquest.

Lucy gripped the glass orb, trying to hide it in the folds of her parka jacket. Solquest lazily pointed his finger towards her. She felt a chilled sensation in her hand as the orb seemed to melt and disappear. With disbelief, she watched as Solquest cupped his palms and the orb reappeared in them. "Ah yes! Now I see what you intended to do. Did you really think that the crystals of Ulum could be removed so easily? Did your conceited brain not tell you that imprisoning Solquest in a shield of energy was an impossible dream?" At the end of each question his voice rose on a high note of accusation. Then it suddenly swooped downwards until it was a low, honeyed murmur that frightened Lucy even more than his shrieking fury. "But how did you reach my island, pretty one? Tell me that. Tell me how you journeyed through the enchanted mist without my knowledge?"

He peered into the orb as if the answers would be revealed in the misty glass but seemed perplexed when he looked back at the terrified girl, whose only reply was her harsh breathing. Then he began to smile, a lazy gloating smile, his eyes watching her as they would a fly desperately buzzing against glass on a window. "Mysteries cannot escape Solquest's scrutiny for long and I will have my answer when next I ask that question. Oh yes, you will answer my question, pretty one, and with my luvenders I will have such fun as the truth reveals itself. But in this moment of renewal, when my world of evil is as fresh as the moment it was first created, there is no time to waste on such triviality. Instead I will show you the strength that lies within this orb. You failed in your mission of vengeance but I, the great Solquest, will not fail. I will show you what you came to do, my pretty one. Watch my power ignite the crystals of Ulum."

When he breathed upon the orb it opened and waves of mist emanated from the exposed crystals. The force of their energy almost flung her from the tribab ledge.

He stared out to sea. His enchanted vision swept over the waves that lapped the jetty at Jutting Toe Pier, over the river of Merrick as it flowed through the centre of South Dock where people danced on the walls and Bella Donna sang songs of joy to celebrate the coming of a New Year.

13

The Festival of Merrick 200

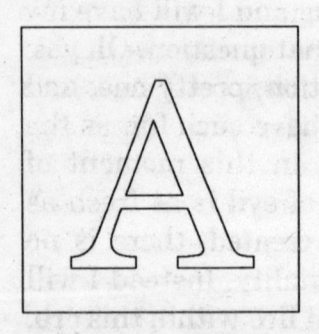

At 10 p.m. on New Year's Eve the committee of Merrick 200 was working feverishly, fighting against time to organise everything for the grand finale at midnight. The mist had delayed all the preparations. Then suddenly, as if fate had kindly decided to lend a hand, the mist lifted, revealing a sparkling clear night and full moon. The captain of the *Triumph* finally made the decision to take the ship out. A volunteer crew of Merrick river-scouts were busy making everything ship-shape.

In the town-centre of Merrick, New Year celebrations were in full swing. Young people danced in the fountain outside the town hall and someone had draped a pair of boxer shorts over the stern-faced statue of Colin Merrick, the town founder. Adults dined in restaurants and drank in pubs or walked towards South Dock with their children. Everyone was in fancy dress. Even the most sedate people wore tinsel wigs or painted their noses white. The GRUB BUG was doing a roaring trade. Old Knees-Up had recovered from his illness and was dressed as a pirate, ferocious with eye-patch and villainous glare.

Kate, in the gauzy harem pants of a genie, whizzed about and the interior of the GRUB BUG, steamy from food sizzling on hotplates, added to the impression that she had just briefly popped out of a bottle.

Don Collins had kindly offered to help her and was handing out containers to the starving hordes crowding around the serving window. For the occasion he was dressed in the magnificent flowing robes of an Arabian sheik, an outfit he had received as a present during his stay in the Middle East. Kate thought he looked splendid. He told her that his life would be perfect if he could bottle her at the end of the night and bring her home.

"Mmmmmm!" wondered Kate, thankful that her daughter was not around to hear him. "What exactly does he mean by that?"

But there was no time to ponder such

ambiguous comments. It was a busy night and going to become even busier.

The youth-club disco was also in full swing, with everyone jumping wildly to the music of Bella Donna and the Quados. Well—almost everyone. Robert Collins scowled at the gyrating figures and wondered what on earth had possessed him to come.

"I'm not going to let *her* spoil my enjoyment," he had vowed earlier in the evening, trying to put his uneasiness to the back of his mind. He had looked at his Sam Sparry costume and realised that he had absolutely no enthusiasm for fancy dress. In a book, *Two Hundred Years of Merrick History*, he had read about Sam Sparry, a scarecrow of an old man who used to dress in a long, ragged coat and a wide-brimmed hat with the flowers and the fruits of the seasons, beautifully created out of cloth and wax, pinned to the brim.

Two hundred years ago, as the *Triumph* sailed into the new port of Merrick, he had beaten his drum in a frenzied rhythm of welcome. Thereafter, every year until his death, he had appeared in Merrick to welcome in the New Year in this fashion.

Last month when Robert told Lucy the story of Sam Sparry she had been so intrigued

The Festival of Merrick 200

by it that she persuaded him to dress as the old man and she would go to Merrick 200 as Elsie Constance.

"Then we'll both be a part of Merrick history," she said.

They had hunted old second-hand clothes shops and junk stalls to find a suitably shabby coat. Lucy was delighted when they discovered a dusty hat with a brim tilting over Robert's eye. In her craft class, she had cut the shapes of flowers and fruit from thick felt material to decorate it. But now, suddenly, the whole charade seemed so ridiculous, especially when he thought of the enormous drum that he had hired out for the night. The Quados had agreed to have it transported to South Dock in the battered transport van that their mother, who was their roadie, drove for them. At midnight Lucy had been supposed to help him beat in the New Year on the drum. But she had turned her back on all that when the H-less Wimp wagged his little finger.

While Robert was brooding in this fashion Paula rang Valerie in hysterics to say that she could not—simply would not—go to Merrick 200 looking like a cross between a marshmallow and a cream doughnut. Robert offered his Sam Sparry outfit to her with a sigh of relief. This offer was gleefully accepted and Paula's father drove over and picked up the outfit.

Jeans and a denim jacket. That would do as well as anything. "I'm going to have a brilliant night," he told his reflection and stormed off to the disco with his friends.

"Where's Rich?" he asked, feeling like a killjoy when he saw his friends in fancy dress. Alan hesitated, looked at the grim face beside him and decided to say nothing about the missing dog. He took the vampire fangs from his mouth and said, "He's been delayed. He's coming along later."

But Rich had not turned up. Nor had Robert's mood improved.

"This place is full of kids," he said, looking at the dancers in disgust.

"They haven't got any younger since last week," replied Paula, reasonably.

By the time 10 p.m. came he was ready to leave. "I can't take any more of this rubbish," he muttered as Bella Donna somersaulted across the stage and Dave the Rave stood on his head with his back to the audience, playing the drums with his heels.

"Come on, Robert. Cheer up. It's New Year's Eve. She'll be back tomorrow," said the ever-tolerant Paula, taking off the Sam Sparry hat.

"It's not that. I just have a feeling that something has happened to Lucy. And every time I try to ring I can't get an answer."

"It's probably something to do with the phone lines out of Merrick. I think the mist is causing all sorts of problems."

To escape the noise they went to the mineral bar and sat on high stools, facing each other. Paula looked anxious and he was quick to notice her uncertainty. "You're worried about Lucy. I know you are."

"I don't know," admitted Paula. "I think I've been deliberately putting it out of my head since I heard she'd left. But where could she be except in Lepping Vale?"

"Yeah! I suppose so. She probably fancied that creep all the time."

"Don't be such a thick-head, Robert. She likes you. I know!"

"How do you know?"

"As a poet I have the gift of being able to pick up such emotional vibrations," replied Paula. "Also, the fact that she blushes three shades deeper than scarlet when she sees you *just* might be an indication of her feelings."

He reflected on this piece of information, brightening up for the first time in two days.

But it was a short-lived flash of pleasure. "Then why would she want to miss tonight?" His confused thoughts kept coming back to the same question.

"I don't know," admitted Paula. "Recently it's been hard to get inside Lucy's mind. She used to close up, as if she was hiding something from us. I should have tried harder... Elsie asked me to take care of her...but the truth is...I didn't really want to know what she was going through. I just wanted to put that whole nightmare behind me."

"Do you think Lucy...?" He abruptly stood up, unable to contemplate the question. "I said something really stupid to her before she went to Lepping Vale. I can't get it out of my head!"

Matt the Brat was doing a guitar solo. It reminded Robert of knives scraping across the surface of a draining board. "I have to get out of here. Are you coming?"

"Oh, I don't know..." Paula looked undecided. The Quados began to play "Marmalade Madness".

"Yes!" she said, wincing. "Let's go. Fast!"

But, just as she was leaving, Bob the Gob saw her and stopped the music. "We are honoured tonight to have the famous songwriter of 'Marmalade Madness' in our midst,

The Festival of Merrick 200

Ms Paula Masterson. Come on, fans! Let's give her a big hand!"

"Ohhhhhhh!" moaned Paula, as she was swept up onto the stage and into the arms of the waiting Quados.

"Good night!" muttered Robert in disgust and left.

Much to his surprise the mist had lifted. It was a crisp night and he breathed deeply, suddenly realising how he had accepted and grown accustomed to the heavy atmosphere that came with such foggy weather. Instead of going home he turned towards South Dock, where families were already beginning to gather. He left the excitement behind, aimlessly walking through the deserted Little Dock area. On a narrow pathway that had been erected around a building site hoarding he heard a familiar bark and the sound of wheels trundling over the wooden slats.

"You gave me a fright," accused Rich. "What are you doing down here? You're supposed to be dressed as a walking scarecrow."

Robert laughed abruptly. "I gave the outfit to Paula. Anyway, what about you? I thought you were supposed to be at the youth club."

"I changed my mind and decided to visit an old friend instead. I'm on my way there now."

"But what are you doing with Spacer?"

"Didn't Alan tell you? I had to collect him. He was back howling at Lucy's place again."

"Damn! Damn! Damn!" Robert leaned his shoulder against the hoarding, where someone had drawn a mural of Little Dock as it would look when all the construction work was finished. "What the hell is that dog up to?"

"Don't ask me. But he was carrying on really weirdly up in Lucy's room. He wouldn't come down, no matter what I did. When I went up after him I found this."

"What is it?" Robert touched the stalactite and drew his hand back quickly as the point pricked his finger.

"Search me. But do you remember that night before Christmas when I was talking to Lucy in Alan's place?"

"Yes." Robert's voice was suddenly guarded. "I wondered what that was all about."

"It was about the zentyre, Solquest, and those crazy pictures she had in her mind."

"What crazy pictures? The day after the mud-slide I *do* remember her saying something about weird pictures and things like that. But she never mentioned it again and every time I asked her about it she choked me off!"

He listened intently as Rich talked about the visions from the island and the red-feathered bird.

"Why didn't she say anything to us?" Robert stared at Rich, amazed and outraged. "Didn't she trust us enough to let us know what was happening?"

"It was nothing to do with trust. All she wanted was to be part of the gang and when you all began to feel hazy about what occurred at the old mill it embarrassed her that she was the only one keeping the whole thing alive."

"But why tell you? What would you know about zentyres?" asked Robert, his curiosity winning out over his ruffled feelings.

"I know more than you realise," Rich replied. "But we haven't time to go into that now." He rummaged in his jacket pocket and pulled something out. "I found this feather lying on the floor of her bedroom."

Robert took the feather from him and clenched it in his fist. "Do you think something's happened to her?" He finally asked the dreaded question.

"We won't know until we ring Lepping Vale," said Rich.

Robert moved impatiently. "I keep trying

but the line has been engaged all day."

"What about ringing another friend? Has she ever mentioned anyone else?"

Robert tried to pick a name from the jumble of conversations that he had had with Lucy about her friends. "There was someone called Jennifer Herrord or Herron..something like that!"

Spacer lay beside the wheelchair, his head turned inquisitively towards the boys as they spoke.

"OK! Let's go find ourselves a phone and ring her." Rich was already moving his chair over the wooden slats.

By the time they located the name Herron with an address in Lepping Vale, Robert was frantic with impatience.

"Hello! Can I help you?" He almost dropped the receiver when a woman's voice answered.

"Is...is Jennifer there?"

"I'm afraid not. Can I give her your name when she comes in?"

"No. I'm a friend of Lucy Constance. I was hoping Jennifer might get Lucy to ring me."

"But Lucy moved last June. Would you like her new address? She writes to Jennifer occasionally."

"Isn't she staying in Lepping Vale at the

moment with H-le..I mean Jon Freeman?" Robert took a deep breath, trying to steady his voice.

"No, I'm afraid you're mistaken. Jon was over here earlier this afternoon and he certainly never mentioned Lucy's name. In fact he's throwing a big party tonight and that's where Jennifer is now. Why don't you ring him there?" The woman began to sound suspicious.

Robert clicked the receiver back into place and stood staring into space. "I can't believe it! I can't believe it!" he muttered over and over again until Spacer licked his hand and butted him on the leg so roughly that life came back into his eyes.

"What is it? What's happened?" Rich grabbed his arm.

"Lucy never went to Lepping Vale." Robert could see the same disbelief turning to realisation on his friend's face.

They stared at each other, helplessly. "Could she possibly have gone to Isealina?"

"There's only one way to find out," said Rich. "Follow me."

The river quickened as it felt the rhythm of the sea drawing it onwards. It flowed past derelict warehouses where rats ran freely under cover of darkness. With a final surge of energy it reached the mouth of the sea and became part of the rolling tide.

On the tip of Jutting Toe Pier, the light from Dr Thorm's house shone like a beacon. The curtains remained undrawn as she sat by her attic window, staring out over the calm sea, listening to the lap of waves against the jetty. There was much to see on this quiet night as the seconds ticked into a new year. She was not surprised when her front doorbell rang.

The two boys and the dog were panting, as if they had raced the length of Jutting Toe Pier. Knowing Richard's speed mania she guessed that they probably had. But it was not exhaustion that made them breathe so rapidly. It was fear. She drew them inside to the warmth of her home and listened to their suspicions. Rich showed her the stalactite. Her eyes narrowed when she saw the smears of dried blood. "Can you climb the stairs to the attic room, Rich?" she asked, noticing the exhaustion on his face.

Rich nodded, steering his chair towards the narrow staircase. They crowded around the attic window.

"Something strange has happened to the

Drowning Mist," Dr Thorm told the boys. "I watched it disappear an hour ago! My uncle was right. It does cover the island of Isealina. If Lucy is there she is in grave danger."

Robert gave a loud AHH! as if someone had punched the breath from his stomach. "The Drowning Mist!" he murmured. "I simply can't believe it."

The moon was a spotlight on the sea, sweeping beams of light over the crown of rocks and the large dome that rose beyond them, visible to their eyes for the first time. An hour before, when the mist lifted, Dr Thorm had been convinced that she was hallucinating. The moon was bright but not bright enough to light the darkness with such a golden glow. She took out her binoculars and turned them towards the horizon. Something moved. Something dark and scurrying, leaping creatures, like large grotesquely-shaped rabbits. They were framed in the light that appeared to radiate from the dome. When her lips closed over the name luvenders, she felt a surge of excitement and laughed like a young girl who has discovered a great secret.

Another figure stepped forth. Dr Thorm's binoculars shook as she tried to steady her hands and he went out of focus. A few deep breaths calmed her. She raised the binoculars once more. Something flashed, a golden glow, like sun caught in a reflection of glass, repeating itself endlessly in mirror images. Symbols of eternity on the robe of a zentyre. Could it possibly be true? It was difficult to see clearly. Yet there was something swaying in the wind, flowers, bronzed leaves throwing out a mellowed sheen, a beautiful sight until their scent reached her and she was overwhelmed by the putrid smell of decaying seaweed.

Dr Thorm had not been aware of moments ticking away as she stared at the hulk of land. The island seemed suspended in time, bathed in a hush of expectation that was disturbed when she heard the frantic ring on her doorbell.

She told them what had happened. Robert shook himself as if he was emerging from a nightmare and began to pace the small attic room, talking in quick jerky sentences. "I often heard Mrs Shine talking about the Drowning Mist but I never...I never thought it had anything to do with Isealina. I'm going over there. I'm going over to that cursed island." It was obvious to Dr Thorm that he blamed himself for Lucy's disappearance.

The Festival of Merrick 200

When they were back downstairs again, Dr Thorm led the way along a corridor to the back of the house. She opened a door and the boys looked down into a boathouse.

"Why did they ever have to discover that the world wasn't flat," moaned Rich as he made his wildly-swinging descent down the stairs. Robert followed, hauling the wheelchair from step to step. The interior of the boathouse smelled of wet wood and oil. A bat swooped from an unseen perch and just as silently disappeared again.

"We'll use my boat," said Dr Thorm, pointing to a small clinker-built boat with an outboard engine.

Rich stared in amazement as she put on a shiny-yellow waterproof jacket and a pair of yellow knee-high wellingtons. "You can't come with us. You'll be in too much danger."

"Listen here, my boy," said the doctor in a voice that brooked no arguments. "I've spent fifty years of my life trying to prove the existence of Solquest. There is no army alive— even the luvenders—with the strength to keep me off that boat." She screwed up her monkey-like face in a gesture of determination. "Are you understanding me, Richard Harrison?"

"Loud and clear," replied Rich.

Dr Thorm opened the up-and-over door. The small boat was suspended above the boathouse floor by an ingeniously arranged pulley system that went into action and swung the boat out onto the jetty cradle when Dr Thorm pulled a lever. The sea was calm but a chill wind whipped their clothes and made their eyes water. Spacer was left behind, whining pathetically and making everyone feel guilty as they closed the boathouse door on him. The boat was poised on the top of the jetty and Rich swung himself from his chair into one of the thwarts. On an impulse he grabbed the stake and placed it behind him, shuddering as his fingers touched the smooth cold object.

The boat moved smoothly along the jetty cradle, pushed by Dr Thorm and Robert. The little hardy woman was obviousy well used to coping with the boat on her own. Soon they were all on board and when Rich looked back he could see the outline of his wheelchair, a solitary object on the jetty. It quickly faded from view. He wondered if he would ever see it again.

He shrugged his shoulders, dismissing such thoughts as Dr Thorm started the outboard motor. When he was younger he had belonged to the Merrick river-scouts and knew how to

The Festival of Merrick 200

handle a boat. Handling a zentyre was a different matter. His nerves were taut as guitar-strings when he looked towards the horizon.

Before him lay the island of mystery, stripped of its mist, yet filled with unseen terrors as the boat headed towards it, cutting through the water like a knife. Sea spray stung his skin and eyes. He pulled his parka jacket tightly around him and tried to stop his teeth from chattering.

"It's not getting any closer," fretted Robert. "It's like those road mirages that disappear as soon as a car gets close to them."

It was impossible to judge the distance of the island. The dome kept looming in front of them as if waiting for their approach. But no matter how fast the boat moved, they still remained the same distance away.

"It's some kind of crazy hallucination," guessed Rich.

"It's no hallucination," replied Robert, grimly. "No matter what happens we'll get there."

It was almost midnight. They had been in the boat for an hour but the elusive island continued to evade them. Then, without warning, the engine of the outboard motor spluttered and cut.

Dr Thorm did not waste any time. She pulled out the emergency oars and passed them to Rich and Robert who were sitting together on the middle thwart. They slotted the oars into the oarlocks and began to row, their elbows moving rhythmically, their breaths released in sharp puffs of energy. Suddenly they heard a chanting voice that chilled the beads of sweat on their foreheads.

*Stones of endless day and night
I will bathe in your light.*

The loud incantation was followed by wild screams, as if the face of evil had been turned towards the moonlight.

"That's Lucy," moaned Robert. The boat rocked crazily as he tried to stand, blindly preparing to swim in the direction of the screams.

"Sit down at once!" ordered Dr Thorm, pulling him back. "There's nothing we can do until we get nearer." Gulping howls of laughter reached across the sea and the people on the boat huddled a little closer. This time the island did not move as they approached. The waves had increased in strength, kicking at the sides of the boat like frantic pony

The Festival of Merrick 200

hooves. Then suddenly the moon faded from view. Without any warning the mist descended. It was impossible to see; even their hands were invisible when they held them in front of their eyes. But Dr Thorm's voice was calm as she urged the two boys not to panic.

They were drifting in a sea of silence. Suddenly a faint whisper of sound reached them. Robert gripped the edge of the thwart and tried to drown out the nauseous humming whine that seemed to be growing louder inside his head. Then he realised that it was coming from the island. The humming noise reached a higher pitch as if wasps, millions of them, circled angrily above them, waiting to attack. He leaned over the edge of the boat and began to retch, violently. Tears ran down his face.

The boat started to spin. Rich clenched his teeth in concentration as he tried to keep rowing. His hands jerked, the oars slipping from his fingers. Then he bowed his head and waited as his world became a clammy silver web that slowly began to tighten around his chest.

14

Trapped in the Mist

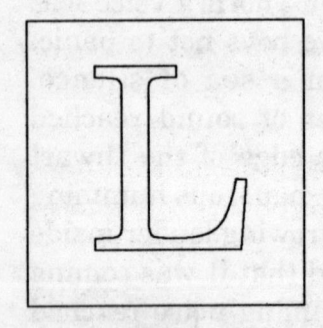

Lucy stood beside Solquest on the ledge surrounding the tribab and felt the power of his enchanted vision stinging her eyes. She blinked and when she looked into the darkness surrounding the island the night had become as bright as day. The boat approaching Isealina stood out in sharp relief. It appeared to be so close to her that she imagined reaching out her hand and touching it. She recognised the boys and gave a despairing cry. They looked cold and frightened. But Dr Thorm's wrinkled face was full of determination as she stared at the island.

Then Lucy was looking beyond the boat and the waves, her gaze sweeping over the sea to Jutting Toe Pier and onwards, over the river as it flowed through Merrick Town. Fairy lights, hanging on either side of South Dock in celebration of Merrick 200, were reflected in dancing strings of colour upon the water. The *Triumph* sailed slowly past. People cheered as fireworks exploded and laser beams drew magnificent shapes in the sky.

Lucy recognised the scene from the final vision that had been revealed to her on the night she rescued the bird from the river. Yet it was different. The disco was over and the young people had arrived on South Dock. Sally and Paula and Valerie did not dance on the wall. They huddled together in a small desolate group with Alan, looking helplessly into the crowds, trying to find the familiar faces of their friends.

"Paula. Help me!" screamed Lucy. The blonde girl, dressed in a ragged coat and crazy hat, and carrying a huge drum in front of her, lifted her head, inquisitively, as if she heard something in the mist that was once again beginning to creep over the river.

"Beat the drum, Paula! Banish the evil of Solquest!" Lucy's call was a defiant cheer that rode across the waves.

Solquest laughed. "The voice of Elsie Constance. A helpless whisper in the mist."

But Paula began to beat the drum, frantically

hammering out a loud rhythm as people stared and moved away from the noise. For an instant the mist paused and hovered on the river.

"Cease your drumming, girl," growled Solquest.

"Keep beating the drum. Lead the people away from the mist," Lucy called once more. But Solquest howled and the defiant beat faltered. It slowly faded away. Paula's hands slumped to her sides.

Lucy watched in horror as the mist rolled over the docks, sinking slowly down upon the roof-tops. Smiling faces were obscured and the joyful sound of celebration was a lost cry, absorbed in the silver vapour.

"They are becoming alarmed," chuckled Solquest. "The music falters. Children begin to cry. What is this mist that winds around our bodies like serpents, they ask? Soon they will know it is the mist of enchantment and their bodies will evaporate like ice thawing in the heat of the morning sun. They will struggle against my power but no one will escape. In time to come, wise women and men will try and find answers to the mystery of Merrick Town, to the disappearance of its population. But they will fail because the answers they seek are earthbound ones. Those who know the answer will remain mute, their spirits trapped in the mist that hangs over my island home. Their cry of knowledge will be lost forever in the silence of zentyre enchantment. And you will join them, my pretty one. You and your friends who dared to think that they could enter Isealina and challenge the might of Solquest."

Suddenly the ledge was filled with a blast of wind that stopped just before it reached Lucy. It poised all around her like a soaring wave, waiting to overpower her. But still it did not move closer. Instead it built up layers of cold air, growing higher and higher until she felt it closing over her head.

Then the mist formed around it and she was watching Solquest and his luvenders from within this haze, unable to move or cry out, unable to break through the enchanted power of the crystals of Ulum as the mist moulded itself around her body. Her breath caught in her throat and her heart was like a tiny trapped creature, fluttering wildly, with no hope of escape. Something flew past her, a flash of red, moving so swiftly that Solquest and his luvenders were not aware of the bird's presence. The Custodian of the Dark Rill looked down sadly upon Lucy and turned her white eyes towards the mist that had surrounded the shore once more.

Beyond the rocks the boat had ceased spinning and drifted uselessly in a dead calm. There was music in the mist. A voice singing words of warning. Something brushed against Rich's cheek. A red shadow began to emerge. A bird who spread her wings in a blanket of protection over them.

"Row swiftly," sang the bird. "There is much evil afoot on this night of the turning year." The air from her beating wings blew away the mist surrounding the high rocks, and the boat, following the passage of the bird, nosed its way through an opening. Within the circle of rocks the sea was calm, and the boat rocked gently. The bird flew low, looking at them from her blank white eyes. For an instant the boys were too dazed to speak.

"Did you just sing words to us?" Robert finally asked.

"Yes, boy. You did indeed hear my word-melody," replied the bird. A drop of blood fell from her chest and shone like a ruby on the bottom of the boat. "Only in my home, the Dark Rill, and on this island of enchantment, are you able to hear my voice." Her music was a plaintive refrain. "My power grows weaker with

Trapped in the Mist

each passing moment. But I cannot leave the girl alone."

"Girl...? Do you mean Lucy?" cried Robert. "What's happened to her? Is...is..." He was unable to finish the sentence.

"Is she safe?" asked Dr Thorm, who, in a remarkably short space of time, seemed to have adjusted to the idea of a bird who sang words of warning. Despite the mystery surrounding them, her face was alive with anticipation.

"The girl tried to steal the crystals of Ulum. But the face of zentyre evil defeated her. Now she is a prisoner of Solquest," replied the bird. "Unless you can steal the crystals and cover their energy she will be removed from us forever. Solquest will then destroy the town of Merrick. Come with me. I will bring you to the girl. But you must act swiftly."

"Does Solquest know we are here?" whispered Dr Thorm.

"Not yet," replied the bird. "He believes that you have already perished in the mist that will soon smother the life from Merrick. All his energy is concentrated on directing the mist across the town. I can distract him from his purpose only for a brief time. Since I was defeated in my great gamble I have lost the strength to overpower him."

"You are in great pain," said Dr Thorm.

The Custodian of the Dark Rill was weak, and growing weaker with every passing second.

"If I do not soon return to the Dark Rill I will die," she agreed. "A bird like me has no room for emotions that twist the heart. Once I am back in the Dark Rill my heart will turn to stone again and my strength will return. But this strange thing called love holds me here until the girl is safe. We must act swiftly. The boy who carries guilt like a knife in his heart will come with me.

"The boy who moves on circles of courage must stay on the boat and be ready to row away immediately the girl is rescued." The song of the bird was becoming faint. "I will lure the zentyre and his army into the tribab. In that instant, boy, you will steal the crystals of Ulum. Close the glass orb over them. Then run with the girl to the shore of Isealina and depart this cursed place."

"Excuse me, bird!" enquired Dr Thorm, firmly. "What about me?"

"Old woman who searches for the truth of zentyre magic, you must stay on the boat. The journey to the tribab is hazardous and your bones will ache."

"Listen here, my fine red-feathered friend.

Trapped in the Mist

Less of this talk about aching bones. I have spent fifty years of my life waiting for such an opportunity. I want to photograph this...this... thing called Solquest. If you think I'm not going where the action is—then think again, warble-mouth!" With that, Dr Thorm stepped from the boat and waded ashore.

"She doesn't mean to be rude but she doesn't like people telling her that she is growing old," explained Rich, apologetically.

The bird smiled. "She has fire in her belly and that will keep her bones young. I will let her go."

As the bird flew away from them, the mist covered the boat once more. Rich shuddered and gripped hands with his friend. Then Robert was ashore, speeding across the stony beach towards the river. When they reached its bank Dr Thorm pulled a small camera from her pocket and pointed it towards the tribab.

"What the hell! Dr Thorm! Put that camera away at once," hissed Robert. "This is no time for photographs."

"Are you suggesting that there is such a time?" hissed back the doctor, sarcastically, and clicked a few more times before shoving the offending camera back into her pocket with the haste of a naughty child hiding sweets. They caught a glimpse of shimmering green stones as they jumped the river.

"How's that for aching bones?" asked Dr Thorm, grimly. Robert was too terrified to respond. He had just seen Lucy outlined in a glow that surrounded her like a second skin, shaping the contours of her body. Her shoulders were hunched and her hands pinned to her sides, as if she was trying to draw herself inwards, away from a force that was slowly crushing her. The luvenders crouched around her, staring at Solquest from eyes that glistened with excitement. Their master held his hands over the open glass orb that he had placed on a jutting crevice in the dome. A silver vapour rose from the crystals and joined the mist of Isealina as it spread outwards from the island and travelled towards Merrick Town.

When Lucy saw Dr Thorm and Robert sheltering beneath the wings of the bird she began to cry, her expression changing from disbelief to relief to terror in the instant of recognition. But no movement came from her body. She looked like a statue that had been dusted in frost.

"Lucy!" Robert whispered. He tried to run forward.

"Stay still!" The warning from the bird was

low but commanding. "She cannot move. And you must not distract the zentyres and his creatures of evil. We must act silently."

When they reached the mulchantus garden the bird soared into the sky and disappeared. The smell from the plants made them recoil but they parted the bronze leaves and hid from view. Upwards they climbed, never pausing, even when they heard deep grunting laughter from the luvenders. Robert moved onto another ledge. He poised, waiting for the signal from the bird. Suddenly he heard a shrill song of attack, coming from inside the tribab.

"Come, zentyre, and listen to the song of the Custodian of the Dark Rill. I will sing of pain and something else that triumphs over all your evil. It is a thing called love."

"What is this I hear?" called Solquest. "A voice from the valley of death."

"I do not hide in a valley," sang the bird. "But in the tribab of the great Solquest."

"This is a dream-vision! You are dead, Custodian! You died when the mist touched Merrick Town. The stake of evil is deep within your heart."

In reply the bird fluttered her wings.

"I will kill this dream-vision," screamed the zentyre. He entered the tribab, followed by his luvenders. Lucy was left alone on the highest ledge of the mulchantus garden.

"Grab the crystals," hissed Dr Thorm. Robert's hands trembled so much that the orb almost fell. But he managed to cover it with his hands and the opening in the glass closed instantly. The mist surrounding Lucy lightened and began to fade. There was no time for words. Lucy beat at the last vaporous wisps with her fists and began to run behind the doctor, frantically jumping from the ledge into the mulchantus garden. High plants closed over their heads. They descended haphazardly, slipping and falling, scratching their legs and arms, but moving, moving all the time towards Rich—and freedom.

But, unknown to Robert, the last luvender to enter the tribab had hesitated at the entrance to glance back at Lucy. Silently the creature waited, smiling in anticipation, until Robert was clear of the garden before springing in a single leap from the tribab and landing on his shoulders. Like a malevolent cat, the luvender clawed at Robert's jacket, scratching at the material and grunting a warning to Solquest. The boy sank to the ground. He could see Lucy hesitating, looking back, her face a mask of terror when she saw what had happened.

Trapped in the Mist

"Keep running, Lucy. Rich is waiting for you!" he screamed. But she was coming back. And so was Dr Thorm. They had almost reached him when Solquest appeared at the entrance to the tribab.

"Did you think you could escape me!" he howled. His fury made him tremble, his mouth was a thin line of vengeance. He stretched out his hands. Instantly Lucy and Dr Thorm froze. Solquest snarled.

"Return my crystals," he ordered the luvender, who still clung to Robert. The glass orb had fallen to the ground but remained unbroken. The luvender quickly scooped it up in his claws and scurried up the ledges. Once more Solquest exposed the crystals. The fading mist strengthened, began slowly to float over the garden to where they stood. Solquest bowed to Dr Thorm. "At least you will die happy, inquisitive woman. You now know that Solquest exists. And, even though you are about to witness my greatest victory, you will never enter it into the final chapter of your book."

15
The Song of Farewell

The Custodian of the Dark Rill watched from high above the tribab. Since she had gambled and lost on the island of Isealina her life had changed in many ways. She had experienced strange emotions of pain and loss and fear. She had spoken of courage to Lucy but its force had not touched her until she saw the boat spinning helplessly within the enchanted mist.

"Foolish humans," she had thought. "What possessed them to follow the girl? They knew the dangers that lie within the mist. What makes them brave everything for another person?" Then she smiled sadly and her wings quivered.

"Ah yes, now I understand this emotion called courage. It comes from love and compassion and greatness of heart. But the kernel of its existence is love. It sent the girl to the river-bank and gave her the strength to pull the stake of evil from my chest. It guided her feet when she climbed to the summit of Tower Rock and it held her firmly as she flew on the wings of trust.

"Courage brought her to the island of Isealina but its strength ran out when she looked upon the face of evil. Now it is the dying whisper of those who came to her rescue. Soon their boat will shatter on the rocks of Isealina and the girl will be alone once more."

The Custodian had tried to silence the voice that told her these things. But it continued to speak to her, soft words of persuasion, drowning out the knowledge that she must return to the Dark Rill and recover her strength.

Against all her instincts of survival, she had gone to the aid of the boys and the old woman. When she guided them through the mist the pain from the stake of evil tore through her chest like an uncoiling length of barbed wire. She had discovered the meaning of courage. But with it came a warning. The Custodian of the Dark Rill had no right to interfere in zentyre enchantment.

Yet, despite this warning, she had entered

the tribab, taunting the zentyre and his army of luvenders with the last of her strength, swooping between the stalactites as Solquest commanded her to his side. Somehow she had managed to resist his voice when he called out to her.

"Come gamble with me, bird. The mist glides over the town of Merrick. How long will it take before my vengeance is complete? A moment—or an hour—or a day? How long will it take before the mist disappears and reveals the sight of empty docklands, empty streets and houses?"

The Custodian quivered with longing, drawn forward by her desire to gamble.

"No," she sang to herself. "No longer will I be controlled by a zentyre's lure."

"No!" she sang again, the word swelling into a note of triumph as she dived towards the zentyre's eyes, wings swirling through the luvender ranks, scattering feathers and confusion among them. Irric, the luvender chief, clawed at her, snarling in fury as her beak grazed his cheek and he fell backwards, hitting his head against the rock. His baleful eyes glittered for an instant before glazing over as he lost consciousness.

Her song trembled with joy when she saw

The Song of Farewell

the humans sprinting towards freedom. They almost made it. Then the luvender sprang and the boy fell. But the girl was free. Why did her feet pause in flight? Why did she return with useless love-words on her lips? Foolish, foolish girl! What strange urges controlled those humans? Then it was too late to wonder. Solquest heard the luvender howl. It had all been in vain. Once again the zentyre and his army had triumphed.

Her blood dripped upon the moss of the tribab. The Dark Rill beckoned her homewards. In the silent flow of the rill she would regain her strength. Her heart would harden into stone and she would continue her timeless flight through eternity. There was nothing more she could do for the humans who stood together on the shore, frozen by the command of Solquest. Within the rocks of Isealina the boy who moved on circles of courage waited for them. Soon he too would be drawn ashore, to be consumed in the power of Solquest.

The bird stared down at the girl with sea-green eyes and sighed. This pain called love troubled her. It made her weak, reluctant to leave this cursed island. But it was time to go.

"Come forward, Lucy Constance," commanded

Solquest. The girl moved away from the boy, who stretched out his hands and tried to hold her back. But the commanding voice was too powerful and she climbed towards the tribab, followed by the boy and the old woman.

"Goodbye, girl," sang the bird.

Lucy looked up into the white eyes of the bird who glided high above. Her own eyes were bright with tears.

"Goodbye," she whispered in her mind. The Custodian heard the words, clearly. "Go back to the Dark Rill before you become too weak to fly. Goodbye, my dear friend."

The bird began to weep. She spread her wings and when she flew above the mist she turned in the direction of the Dark Rill. High pure notes broke through the silence of Isealina as she began her song of farewell.

Her song rose higher, sweet and pure as the ringing chimes of a tuning fork, so high that it seemed to shatter the stars. And for an instant that was what appeared to happen. The sky was full of fire, as if a volcano had erupted on the summit of the tribab, and arched itself into a magnificent spectrum. Then it broke apart and became many small deadly flames. The song of the Custodian had opened the flood-gates of the Dark Rill and released the spectrums of vice. Through the air they flew with a great keening wail of freedom. The luvenders screamed as flames of many colours licked the summit of the tribab and scorched towards them.

They began to run, gibbering in terror as they darted along the mulchantus ledges, scurrying through the thick-stemmed plants and crouching between the bronze leaves. But the plants that nurtured the luvenders, gave them food and drink, were unable to protect them from the fury that blazed around them. Snakes of flame moved between the ledges, keening promises of revenge on the servants of Solquest.

In that moment in time, that brief moment of freedom before their murderous fire of vengeance was extinguished forever, the spectrums of vice destroyed the luvenders. Solquest watched in horror as his creatures fell, their bodies consumed in an inferno that flashed like an exploding sun over the island of Isealina.

The spectrums of vice once again formed together into a single flame that flew like a radiant arrow towards Solquest. Within the spectrum he recognised the faces of all those people who had responded to his call. Those who had sought the prizes of glory and wealth by becoming his followers on earth. His power was no match for the pent-up fury of those who had been trapped in the timeless flow of the Dark Rill. Their hatred for the zentyre was a torch that would overwhelm and destroy him. Solquest moaned in terror. He grabbed the crystals of Ulum, lifted them from the glass orb and pressed them against his chest. "Crystals of Ulum. I draw all your energy to me. Protect me from the wrath of the spectrums of vice."

Instantly the mist that covered the sea and the town of Merrick disappeared. It was swept away from Lucy and Robert, from Dr Thorm, from the shores of Isealina so that Rich, waiting in trepidation in its depths, was suddenly able to see what was happening. The island of Isealina was an inferno but in the centre of the leaping, keening flame he could see a long silver column that formed a shield against the heat that engulfed it.

Robert and Lucy began to run, stopped and ran back for Dr Thorm who was crouched on one knee taking photographs.

"Come on! Come on!" screamed Rich. Even as he watched, the whirlwind of fire was beginning to fade. Then darkness descended

The Song of Farewell

on the island as the spectrum's brief flight of freedom was quenched forever. Rich looked upwards towards the column of mist, glowing with a silver sheen, thick as marble, and as impenetrable. There was danger in it. He could feel it in every bone in his body.

"Come on, Lucy. Run! Run!" His voice faltered as he watched the silver cloud splitting in two.

Solquest stepped free and looked out over his desolate island. The mulchantus garden was a charred forest of blackened stalks. Grey dust marked the spot where his luvenders fell. The spectrums of vice were just a pall of drifting smoke, settling over the waves.

"But you still have not defeated Solquest!" he screamed. He raised his hands in the air.

Solquest's voice echoed over the island. In the boat Rich shuddered. The footsteps of his friends faltered as they raced towards the sea. He reached behind him and his fingers closed over the stalactite that had pierced the chest of the bird. He let it rest in the palm of his hand.

Solquest's eyes swept the shore towards the boat and came to rest on Rich. "So, we meet again, Richard." The zentyre no longer screamed. His voice was honey, sliding over the waves, sweet words that Rich remembered so well. The last time he heard them he was a trembling boy of thirteen who had been woken from his midnight slumber to learn the secrets of zentyre enchantment.

"Come, Richard, and join your friends. Solquest is lonesome. He needs new blood on his island of Isealina. I offered you a wonderful gift once before and you foolishly refused it. This time you have no choice. Come to me, Richard. Come and breathe the air of Isealina. Come and I will teach you the mesmerising chants that carry my magic into the dark places of the mind."

Lucy screamed, "Don't listen to him, Rich. We can defeat him." But she stopped running towards the boat when Solquest's eyes pierced her back and she tumbled forward, as if pushed by an invisible hand.

In that instant, while Solquest was distracted, Rich arched his arm back over his shoulder and took aim. The stalactite glided above the rocks of Isealina and the charred garden of mulchantus, and flew towards the tribab entrance where Solquest stood. The symbol of a golden sun rising through eternity glowed radiantly on his white robe but it was splashed with zentyre blood as the stalactite entered the chest of Solquest. He howled once,

The Song of Farewell

outraged, disbelieving, then slumped forward, his body spilling from ledge to ledge in a fluid, almost langorous movement.

Rich gripped Lucy by the hand, hauling her on board. Robert lifted Dr Thorm through the shallow waves. His hair was sleeked back from his forehead and his brown eyes were luminous with fear as he climbed into the boat.

Robert tried to start the engine, hoping against hope that he would hear the throbbing sound. But although the engine spluttered once it quickly died away and he was forced to grab the oars.

Rich slumped helplessly in the bow of the boat, staring at the palms of his hands. "I'll never again be able to hold a javelin without thinking about this," he whispered in a voice that spoke of many nightmares to come.

"Oh, you will! You will!" Dr Thorm wrapped her arms around him and tried to comfort him. Lucy took one of the oars from Robert, moving into the rower's thwart beside him. There was no false light to guide them but the moon shone from a clear sky and dappled the waves as they rowed in unison, pulling strongly on the oars. A cold, raw wind blew around them but they were sweating with exertion and exhaustion as they turned the boat in the direction of home. When the rocks of Isealina disappeared into the night, Rich finally ceased to tremble. The journey home was short. Within a half an hour they could see the blurred outlines of Jutting Toe Pier.

"We'd better stop and collect Spacer," said Robert as the sound of faint, anxious barks floated over the waves. "Then we'll row down-river to South Dock. We have many reasons for celebrating Merrick 200."

"Don't forget my wheels," ordered Rich as the boat was brought to a gentle halt beside the pier.

Robert ran up the jetty and grabbed Rich's chair. The barks from the boathouse had reached a crescendo and, when he opened the door, Spacer almost knocked him over with the force of his welcome.

"Fold that tongue back into your mouth, you slob," said Robert, dropping to his knees and hugging the quivering body. The boathouse was a dark and private place where he could cry in secret. Spacer licked Robert's hand then stood still as the boy wept into his thick, black coat. Then they were racing back down the jetty and Spacer almost capsized the boat as he bounded onto Lucy's lap and licked her face. Eventually they managed to calm the dog. When the wheelchair was folded and stored, Rich changed places with Lucy, hoisting himself into the thwart beside Robert and beginning to row. As they moved downriver they could see the lights on South Dock in the distance.

Suddenly they heard a splash and felt a gentle bump against the side of the boat. When Lucy leaned forward and stared into the water it was impossible to see anything. But her fingers touched something, feathers, sleek and wet. Her hands curled into a cradle and she lifted the Custodian of the Dark Rill on board.

"She must have followed us from Isealina. Now she is too weak to fly any longer," whispered Lucy. There was a lump in her throat as she rested the bird against her jacket and caressed the tiny, wizened face.

Lashless lids opened. "I did it for you, girl." The bird's song rattled deep in her throat. "You wept over me once and taught me how to love. So many emotions spring from love that they have stopped my heart returning to stone." She gave a deep shuddering sigh. Her eyelids closed forever over the white eyes. The wound in her chest disappeared.

"She is dead," cried Lucy. "She is no longer the Custodian of the Dark Rill. She knew this would happen when she released the spectrums of vice." Lucy bent her head and crooned a song of love to the bird. Then she smoothed the wings of the Custodian and rested her body on the river where they had first met. She watched the red feathers swirl slowly then disappear beneath the water.

"You must not grieve for her, Lucy," said Dr Thorm. "The bird is at peace. She made her decision willingly because she loved you. Now you must also be at peace."

In the distance they could hear a drum beating. The sound added strength to the boys' arms. Everyone looked back once towards Isealina. Darkness closed around them and refused to give up its secrets. But they imagined the island, rising from the sea, washed in the deceptive beauty of moonlight. They shivered and turned their faces resolutely towards South Dock and the glowing lights that welcomed them home to Merrick Town.

Epilogue

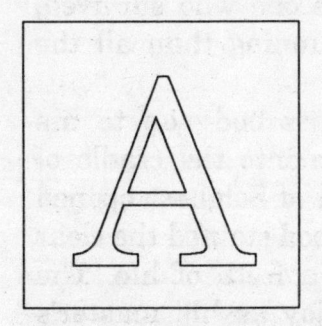

An eerie silence settled over Isealina. Scattered crystals lay beneath the dead ash of the mulchantus garden. Within the tribab of Isealina the luvender called Irric moved swiftly from the shelter of the rock-slab. His head ached from the blow it had received when the custodian swooped towards him. Her beak had drawn blood from his cheek.

He swayed, feeling dizzy, as he climbed the steps of the tribab. When he emerged from the passageway he screeched with disbelief as he looked down upon the island's devastation. The end of his world had arrived.

He saw his master, Solquest, his body twisted in agony as he lay beside the river bank. A stake of evil was embedded in his heart. Even when Irric removed the stake, the zentyre's eyes did not open, nor did his pulse flicker with life.

"Come back to me, master," cried the luvender. "Your army of luvenders has been destroyed but I, Irric, the one who survived, am stronger and more cunning than all the others."

Irric lifted his master's body on to his shoulder and carried him into the cradle of eternal youth. The wound of Solquest opened to the flow of the river. Blood stained the clear water and it erupted in a froth of life. The luvender wept tears of joy as his master's fingers uncurled and reached towards the three green stones of Isealina.

Praise for
When the Luvenders Came to Merrick Town

"Magic and monsters are most chilling when they insinuate themselves into everyday life. That's why [this book] is such an enthralling read."

The Irish Times

"Well written, with a nice mixture of magic, fantasy and adventure."

Evening Herald

"It's a totally gripping fantasy tale."

RTE Guide

"This is a wonderful book, that children of all ages will enjoy, and that will keep them entranced for many hours."

Southside Gazette

"I think the *Luvenders* is the best real fantasy I have ever read...I wanted to keep reading and reading and reading. It was really gripping."

Laura Reece, young reviewer, *Books Ireland*

Soon to be translated into Italian!

Praise for
Luvenders at the Old Mill

"This is an outstanding book which displays great knowledge of young people."
The Irish Guide to Children's Books, 1991

"June Considine has another enthralling fantasy with *Luvenders at the Old Mill*. It's the sequel to last year's bestseller and much swopped in our house."
Evening Press

"Miss Considine writes powerfully about the ancient evil of Solquest...She seems to know the minds of fourteen-year-olds."
The Irish Times

"Greatly enjoyed by those who read it."
Books Ireland

"I would recommend this highly if you like getting absorbed in a book."
Madeleine, young reviewer for *Books Ireland*

Soon to be translated into Italian!

Children's Poolbeg Books

Author	Title	ISBN	Price
Banville Vincent	Hennessy	1 85371 132 2	£3.99
Beckett Mary	Orla was Six	1 85371 047 4	£2.99
Beckett Mary	Orla at School	1 85371 157 8	£2.99
Comyns Michael	The Trouble with Marrows	1 85371 117 9	£2.99
Considine June	When the Luvenders came to Merrick Town	1 85371 055 5	£4.50
Considine June	Luvenders at the Old Mill	1 85371 115 2	£4.50
Considine June	Island of Luvenders	1 85371 149 7	£4.50
Corcoran Clodagh ed.	Baker's Dozen	1 85371 050 4	£3.50
Corcoran Clodagh ed.	Discoveries	1 85371 019 9	£4.99
Cruickshank Margrit	SKUNK and the Ozone Conspiracy	1 85371 067 9	£3.99
Cruickshank Margrit	SKUNK and the Splitting Earth	1 85371 119 5	£3.99
Daly Ita	Candy on the DART	1 85371 057 1	£2.99
Daly Ita	Candy and Sharon Olé	1 85371 159 4	£3.50
Dillon Eilís	The Seekers	1 85371 152 7	£3.50
Dillon Eilís	The Singing Cave	1 85371 153 5	£3.99
Duffy Robert	Children's Quizbook No.1	1 85371 020 2	£2.99
Duffy Robert	Children's Quizbook No.2	1 85371 052 0	£2.99
Duffy Robert	Children's Quizbook No.3	1 85371 099 7	£2.99
Duffy Robert	The Euroquiz Book	1 85371 151 9	£3.50
Ellis Brendan	Santa and the King of Starless Nights	1 85371 114 4	£2.99
Henning Ann	The Connemara Whirlwind	1 85371 079 2	£3.99
Henning Ann	The Connemara Stallion	1 85371 158 6	£3.99
Hickey Tony	Blanketland	1 85371 043 1	£2.99
Hickey Tony	Foodland	1 85371 075 X	£2.99
Hickey Tony	Legendland	1 85371 122 5	£3.50
Hickey Tony	Where is Joe?	1 85371 045 8	£3.99
Hickey Tony	Joe in the Middle	1 85371 021 0	£3.99
Hickey Tony	Joe on Holiday	1 85371 145 4	£3.50
Hickey Tony	Spike & the Professor	1 85371 039 3	£2.99
Hickey Tony	Spike and the Professor and Doreen at the Races	1 85371 089 X	£3.50
Hickey Tony	Spike, the Professor and Doreen in London	1 85371 130 6	£3.99
Kelly Eamon	The Bridge of Feathers	1 85371 053 9	£2.99
Lavin Mary	A Likely Story	1 85371 104 7	£2.99
Lynch Patricia	Brogeen and the Green Shoes	1 85371 051 2	£3.50
Lynch Patricia	Brogeen follows the Magic Tune	1 85371 022 9	£2.99
Lynch Patricia	Sally from Cork	1 85371 070 9	£3.99
Lynch Patricia	The Turfcutter's Donkey	1 85371 016 4	£3.99
MacMahon Bryan	Patsy-O	1 85371 036 9	£3.50
McCann Sean	Growing Things	1 85371 029 6	£2.99
McMahon Sean	The Poolbeg Book of Children's Verse	1 85371 080 6	£4.99
McMahon Sean	Shoes and Ships and Sealing Wax	1 85371 046 6	£2.99
McMahon Sean	The Light on Illancrone	1 85371 083 0	£3.50
McMahon Sean	The Three Seals	1 85371 148 9	£3.99
Mullen Michael	The Viking Princess	1 85371 015 6	£2.99
Mullen Michael	The Caravan	1 85371 074 1	£2.99
Mullen Michael	The Little Drummer Boy	1 85371 035 0	£2.99
Mullen Michael	The Long March	1 85371 109 8	£3.50
Mullen Michael	The Flight of the Earls	1 85371 146 2	£3.99
Ní Dhuibhne Eilís	The Uncommon Cormorant	1 85371 111 X	£2.99

Author	Title	ISBN	Price
Ní Dhuibhne Eilís	Hugo and the Sunshine Girl	1 85371 160 8	£3.50
Ó hEithir Breandán	An Nollaig Thiar	1 85371 044 X	£2.99
Ó Faoláin Eileen	The Little Black Hen	1 85371 049 0	£2.99
Ó Faoláin Eileen	Children of the Salmon	1 85371 003 2	£3.99
Ó Faoláin Eileen	Irish Sagas and Folk Tales	0 90516 971 9	£3.95
Quarton Marjorie	The Cow Watched the Battle	1 85371 084 9	£2.99
Quarton Marjorie	The Other Side of the Island	1 85371 161 6	£3.50
Quinn John	The Summer of Lily and Esme	1 85371 162 4	£3.99
Ross Gaby	Damien the Dragon	1 85371 078 4	£2.99
Schulman Anne	Children's Book of Puzzles	1 85371 133 0	£3.99
Snell Gordon	Cruncher Sparrow High Flier	1 85371 100 4	£2.99
Snell Gordon	Cruncher Sparrow's Flying School	1 85371 163 2	£2.99
Stanley-Higel Mary	Poolbeg Book of Children's Crosswords 1	1 85371 098 9	£2.99
Stanley-Higel Mary	Poolbeg Book of Children's Crosswords 2	1 85371 150 0	£3.50
Swift Carolyn	Bugsy Goes to Cork	1 85371 071 7	£3.50
Swift Carolyn	Bugsy Goes to Limerick	1 85371 014 8	£3.50
Swift Carolyn	Bugsy Goes to Galway	1 85371 147 0	£3.99
Swift Carolyn	Irish Myths and Tales	1 85371 103 9	£2.99
Swift Carolyn	Robbers on TV	1 85371 033 4	£2.99
Swift Carolyn	Robbers on the Streets	1 85371 113 6	£3.50
Traynor Shaun	A Little Man in England	1 85371 032 6	£2.99
Traynor Shaun	Hugo O'Huge	1 85371 048 2	£2.99
Traynor Shaun	The Giants' Olympics	1 85371 088 1	£2.99
Traynor Shaun	The Lost City of Belfast	1 85371 164 0	£3.50
	The Ultimate Children's Joke Book	1 85371 168 3	£2.99

While every effort is made to keep prices low, it is sometimes necessary to increase prices at short notice. Poolbeg Press Ltd reserves the right to show new retail prices on covers which may differ from those previously advertised in the text or elsewhere.

All Poolbeg books are available at your bookshop or newsagent or can be ordered from:

**Poolbeg Press Knocksedan House
Forrest Great Swords Co Dublin
Tel: 01 407433 Fax: 01 403753**

Please send a cheque or postal order (no currency) made payable to Poolbeg Press Ltd.

Allow 80p for postage for the first book, plus 50p for each additional book ordered.